PRAISE FOR *ALGORITHMS*

"The third installment in the Seventh Flag trilogy, *Algorithms*, perfectly combines the excitement of a post-apocalyptic thriller with a poignant coming-of-age story featuring an engaging heroine facing a very different 'American Dream.' Indeed, a page-turner . . . an important read for any citizen concerned about the reality of where our culture wars and politics are taking American society. In the final analysis, a convincing argument for optimism"

—**Laura Payne, PhD**, Dean, Jimmy D. Case College
of Literature, Arts, and Social Sciences Sul Ross
State University

"Big questions, grand themes, and prophetic warnings: all these characterize *Algorithms*. Another first-rate novel by Sid Balman, Jr."

—**Robert Zorn**, Award-Winning Author of *Cemetery John: The Undiscovered Mastermind of the Lindbergh Kidnapping*

"Sid Balman's Algorithms is a thrilling climax to his cross-generational west Texas saga. In the dystopian future, his tale of a technological and societal collapse is stunning, and, unfortunately not-implausible. The resilience of his heroes and the indigenous communities he depicts gives me some hope for our current times."

—**Chris Wolz**, CEO of Forum One

PRAISE FOR *MURMURATION*

"When a young Somali immigrant is confronted by hatred, it's no surprise that he will rebel against the society that rejects him. *Murmuration* is a fast-paced thriller that captures the horror of the Somali refugee crisis and brings that horror home to America. It is a story of fear, revenge, compassion, and ultimately redemption. Sid Balman Jr. writes about the global threat of ISIS with the confidence and authority of someone who has witnessed it firsthand. This novel is a compelling glimpse into a dangerous world."

—Clifford Garstang, author of *What the Zhang Boys Know* and *The Shaman of Turtle Valley*

"The book we should all be reading right now! *Murmuration* is a work of absorbing historical detail but also a multilayered story of love, honor, loss, and the plague of radicalism. Sid Balman Jr. carries us from West Texas into the battleground of Mogadishu and from refugee camps in Kenya to suburban Minnesota, giving us a deeper understanding of our global struggle with radicalism. Nothing is ever what it seems."

—Donatella Lorch, award-winning war correspondent for the *New York Times*, *Newsweek*, and NBC News

"Mr. Balman has written what I consider one of the Great American Novels of the 21st century. In *Murmuration*, the second novel in the Seventh Flag trilogy, he has turned on its head the traditional notions of heroism, patriotism, loyalty, and gender. He introduces us to a new American icon in Ademar Zarkan, a Syrian Muslim woman raised in West Texas, a West Point graduate, and a US Army sniper who struggles to reconcile her roles as an assassin and a mother. Zarkan's life is defined by her relationship with Charlie Christmas, the Somali translator she meets in war-torn Mogadishu, and Prometheus Stone, a lapsed Jew and an Army captain. The unlikely trio make a perilous journey from Africa to Minnesota with Christmas's son, Amir, who falls prey to the siren song of violent radicalism and ends up sharing a prison cell with a hardened white supremacist. Balman weaves three decades of experience with conflict and extremism into a heartbreaking tale of diaspora and displacement that has defined the saga of so many migrants to the United States. As one who has made that journey, I urge all my countrymen and women—whether Somali or American—to read *Murmuration*."

—**Mohamed Abdirizak**, foreign minister of Somalia

"With the familiarity born of personal experience in conflict, Sid Balman Jr. takes the reader inside the purgatory of an African refugee camp, lets the reader hear the snap of a passing bullet and feel the satisfaction of a sniper's kill shot. He chronicles the turmoil in the head of a young Somali lured by unexpected sexual access and the calls to violence of an imam preaching not the Koran but nihilism. Torments inflicted by white nationalists and gang violence inside American prisons confront his protagonists. Sid is at his best capturing nature's challenge and appeal, from a sandstorm's bite to the horrors of a crocodile's strike. More than a good read, the novel presents the backstory to today's headlines."

—**US ambassador James Bishop** (ret.)

PRAISE FOR *SEVENTH FLAG*

"*Seventh Flag* tells a tough-as-Texas multigenerational story. A soul-searching read that should make people think twice about what our conscience and families might ask of us in the end. Balman expertly guides readers through the paths that people take to become evil, and the horrific choices that must be made to fight loved ones who have trod that path. A must-read . . . a fun white-knuckle ride that has honest tension and high stakes."
—**Jef Rouner**, *Houston Chronicle*

"To me, what made this book stand out was the core belief that "we are all Americans" together in this battle against extremism, racial bigotry, and hate, in whatever form it may take."
—*Readers' Favorite* 5-star review

"At precisely the moment when our diverse and multi-ethnic nation needs a spiritual lift, Sid Balman gives us a portrait of the complex racial and generational relations that define who we really are as Americans. You can smell the creosote of the desert and taste the huevos rancheros in this tale of West Texas. A splendid account of what being American is all about. A rich portrait useful to us all."
—**Mike McCurry**, former White House press secretary

"*Seventh Flag* is a thriller with action that heightens in the second half of the book, which opens after the events of 9/11. The narrative has the quality of reportage, rife with anecdotes and historical asides, and deals with such hot-button issues as religion, patriotism, and sexuality. Balman dives into political parties, the dark corners of the Internet, and the rise of hate groups and terrorist cells."
—**Jennifer Levin**, *Santa Fe New Mexican*

"Think you know what shapes Texas? Sid Balman's tale of a Seventh Flag over Texas will rattle what you think. This saga of a generational partnership "as unlikely as the idea of a United States" is rooted in a true event before the Civil War that led to Texas, of all places, being home to more Muslim Americans than any other state."

—**Mark Stein**, *New York Times* bestselling author of *How the States Got Their Shapes*

"Sid Balman's story comes alive through sympathetic characters and description of places so nuanced I imagined I could almost feel again the scratchy grey wool of the West Point uniform. Anyone paying attention to the global struggle with radicalism will come away with a much keener understanding of the humans who fall prey, the context that claims them, and the necessity to tackle this challenge with more finesse than we currently muster."

—**Kimberly C. Field**, brigadier general USA (ret.)

"*Seventh Flag* is a book about pluralism. It's also a book about the tensions increasingly found in pluralistic societies, and about the plague of violent radicalism, including white supremacy and ISIS, that sweeps across the novel's world and two families over four generations."

—**Emma Sarappo**, *Washington City Paper*

ALGORITHMS

ALGORITHMS

A NOVEL

SID BALMAN JR.

BOOK 3 IN THE SEVENTH FLAG TRILOGY

SPARKPRESS

Published by SparkPress, a BookSparks imprint,
A division of SparkPoint Studio, LLC
Phoenix, Arizona, USA, 85007
www.gosparkpress.com

Published 2023
Printed in the United States of America
Print ISBN: 978-1-68463-208-4
E-ISBN: 978-1-68463-209-1
Library of Congress Control Number: 2023900091

Title page whale illustration by Yvette Contois, 2022, yvettecontois.com
Interior design by Tabitha Lahr

Mary Oliver's *Wild Geese* reprinted with the permission of her estate.

For the Free People of West Texas

It is decadent in every way. And like most decadent things, it reaches its fullest flower at its rottenest point, which is the present.

—ERNEST HEMINGWAY,
Death in the Afternoon

KEY PLAYERS

ADEMAR ZARKAN. . . . . Leader of the Free People of
West Texas
CROCKETT LAWS II
(DEUCE). . . . . Ademar's husband, grandson
of the founder of Dell City
ARWEN LAWS. . . . . Their granddaughter
STAR . . . . Arwen's dog
TAMERLANE LAWS III
(T3) . . . . Arwen's uncle
PROMETHEUS STONE . . . . Army Ranger, rabbi,
Ademar's captain in Somalia
CHARLIE CHRISTMAS . . . . Ademar's translator in Somalia
AMIIR . . . . Charlie's son
NOAH . . . . Stone's son
AMINA. . . . . Stone's Somali American wife
MOTHER . . . . Leader of the Sisterhood
BETTY AND ANNIE
(SUCCUBUS AND HECATE) . . . . Sisterhood warriors
WHITE EAGLE . . . . Lakota Sioux shaman, leader
of the Mountain Tribes of the
West
RED THUNDER. . . . . White Eagle's wife
MAWIYA . . . . Leader of the Raramuri
(Tarahumara)
CABA. . . . . Mawiya's best friend
NICO POMPADOR . . . . American president
ANONYMOUS . . . . Hacker group

KEY LOCATIONS

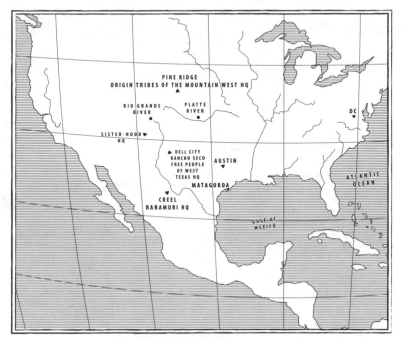

FIG.1 MAP US

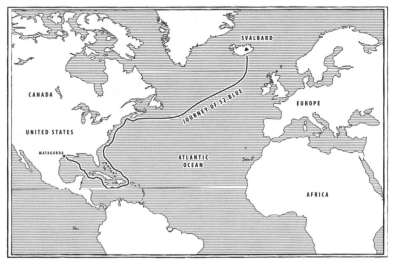

FIG.2 SVALBARD

CHAPTER 1

2039: AFTER THE FALL

The spray of mist comes first, an eruption of white foam forty feet high. Then the leviathan, the last remaining blue whale, transmitting at fifty-two hertz a deep-sea summons to her lost mate, her lost purpose on a path as wide as the ocean. The world's loneliest aquatic bagpiper at fifty-two hertz all day long. The perfect metaphor for life after the Fall of mankind in 2037. 52 Blue, as scientists named her when she was tagged before the Fall, propels her four hundred thousand pounds from the Gulf of Mexico with a single elegant whip of her tail. The largest mammal to live on planet earth, with a tongue weighing as much as an elephant, levitates her full one-hundred-foot body above the water. She twists in midair, impossibly acrobatic, flashing her white belly, a single fin, and what—from the beach of Matagorda Island less than three hundred feet away—could only be a smile, the smile of a mother seeing her newborn for the first time. And 52 Blue's heart, the entirety of her four-hundred-pound heart, belongs to one creature and one creature only: Arwen Laws, the redheaded thirteen-year-old girl on the beach with the inexplicable telepathic connection to the whale and the razor-sharp blade of an Uncle Henry Hawkbill hard against her throat.

Mother, the high priestess of the Sisterhood, smiles and squeezes Arwen's puerile left breast with her free hand. But the blade of the knife in her other hand doesn't move.

"First the whale," Mother whispers in Arwen's ear. "Then you."

A dozen of Mother's trusted acolytes from the Sisterhood, a sect of women warriors who have ruled a chunk of Arizona and New Mexico since the Fall, since the end of everything, form a phalanx around their figurehead. In one voice, as the whale drops back into the water, they raise the battle cry of the Sisterhood, a shrill, bone-chilling ululation like the howl of something from Hell.

This is the moment of truth, that split second when a matador stands on his toes, sword poised over the shoulder of a defeated bull, and the crowd is as silent as a drifting feather. The moment of truth before the blade pierces the soft spot between the bull's powerful shoulder blades, down into his heart, and man and bull—for a violent, beautiful moment—become one.

Like her fellow leaders in the dominant fiefdoms that coalesced after the Fall, when technology and leadership run amok decimated the delicate tapestry of the real and virtual world, Mother has sought only one thing since the Fall: the algorithms. In an act of stunning bravery and cunning, a lone oceanographer just before the Fall is said to have tapped into the undersea cables that transported the ones and zeroes that encompassed the essence of modern humanity. As legend would have it, Hannah Spencer, a marine biologist at the US Department of Energy, somehow managed to store everything—every algorithm, every question, every answer, every memory, and the power to unleash the world's nuclear arsenals—in hard drives she embedded deep under the back fin of 52 Blue. The Holy Grail that the self-ruled sects, fiefdoms, and tribes have sought is finally within Mother's reach.

A dot of red light appears on Mother's chest, and the crack of a gunshot pierces the silence. An acolyte dives in front of the Sisterhood leader just in time to stop the 170-grain round, which rips a dime-shaped hole in her lower back and blasts a puddle of viscera out of her abdomen like a nest of serpents. The phalanx of warriors tightens around Mother, and she draws the knife across Arwen's throat with enough pressure to draw a thin line of blood, but not enough to kill. And Mother knows that the shooter will never risk the life of Arwen Laws, granddaughter of Ademar Laws, former US Army sniper and leader of the Free People of West Texas.

"*Allahu Akbar*," *God is great*, shouts Charlie Christmas, the Somali refugee and lifelong friend to Ademar, who, like Charlie, was raised a Muslim. "One hundred and seventy yards. Not bad, Ranger."

"For shit," Ademar replies and chambers another round into her Henry lever-action .30-30, the mythical ranch gun she first learned to shoot as a farm girl sixty years ago in the tiny West Texas town of Dell City. "Now what?"

A battle cry pierces the silence. Dust rises from the distance, and out of it emerges a single rider, bareback astride a horse with red handprints on its flanks.

"White Cloud," Ademar whispers.

All stop. All hold their breath and turn to look at White Cloud, Ademar's ally and a ninety-year-old Lakota Sioux shaman of the Origin Tribes in the Mountain West. The old man seems transformed into the warrior of his youth, war paint on his face and body, feathered, beaded lance in one hand and reins in the other. The horse rises on its back legs and paws the air with its hooves. White Cloud lets out the ancient battle cry of the Sioux, leans low over the horse's neck, and charges.

CHAPTER 2

BEFORE THE FALL

Once upon a time, there was a *united* states of America. It was a nation founded on a set of principles that enshrined freedom for all people. Imperfect, often hypocritical, and frequently anything but fair and equal, this nation of immigrants and Indigenous people was resilient and endured well into the twenty-first century. There were times when it teetered on the brink of failure: the Civil War, the Great Depression, World War II, Watergate, and the cultural brawls of the 1960s. But the lady with the torch in New York Harbor remained standing—defiant, proud, welcoming.

And nowhere embodied this idea, this grand experiment, like Dell City, Texas, population 413.

And no families walked that walk like the Lawses and the Zarkans.

Deep in the high desert of West Texas eighty miles east of El Paso, Jack Laws helped found Dell City in the early 1950s on an educated guess by his wife, Marcelina, an agronomist and one of those Texas women who had a way with a petticoat and a .30-30. She advised him to build the farm on top of the massive Bone Spring–Victorio Peak Aquifer, and, as with most things, Marcelina was right. The liquid gold that flowed into the ground from the snowmelt just across the border in the Sacramento Mountains of New Mexico transformed the dust of Dell City into an agricultural oasis of cantaloupes, cotton, onions, tomatoes, chili peppers, and sorghum. A Texas Supreme Court ruling in 2012 on the regulations over extraction redefined water rights in the American West and netted a fortune for the Lawses when they struck a deal with the city of El Paso that sent millions of gallons annually to the parched and growing city.

Ali Zarkan, like Jack, fought and killed Japanese in the battles of the Western Pacific during World War II. Jack served as a gunner on a troop transport ship and lost his right thumb to 7.7 mm round from the nose-gun of a Japanese Zero. Ali lost his soul, and his faith in Allah, somewhere amid the blood-soaked hand-to-hand battles in the steamy jungles, where the pop of a bullet into a chest or the sucking sound of a trench knife pulled from a soldier's gut transformed him from an idealistic young man into an aimless, Godless zombie roaming West Texas making enough money in bare-knuckled fights or picking cotton to keep him in tequila and whores.

Ali had family in Texas due to President Franklin Pierce's decision in 1853 to create the US Army Camel Corps. Secretary of War Jefferson Davis felt it was a stroke of genius to ship thousands of camels and Arab handlers from the Middle East and North Africa to the port of Indianola, 140 miles south of Houston. The dromedaries, which required little water and could live on the indigenous desert vegetation, would be perfect as pack animals for the US Cavalry in the desert Southwest. But the experiment ultimately failed with the onset of the Civil War, a change in the administration, and the reticence of the US Cavalry toward the unruly camels.

The dromedaries and their handlers stayed, among them Ali's great-grandfather, Mustafa Zarkan.

That ripple in the universe, that bit of serendipitous circumstance, found a drunk Jack squared off with three equally drunk Mexican *vaqueros*, switchblades in hand, at the bar of the El Recreo cantina in Juarez. Were it not for Ali, sipping mezcal in a dark corner and enjoying the glimmer of air from a creaky overhead fan, Jack might have been just another dead gringo on the floor of a Mexican dive bar. Perhaps it was the tequila, or perhaps Ali's death wish and guilt over his lapsed faith, or perhaps just the magnetism of a good fight against great odds, but Ali stepped in, and together they prevailed in a flurry of broken bottles and shattered bones. It was a moment that defined both men and cemented a partnership that brought prosperity and vision to their lives and to the lives of their offspring. Side by side in Dell City, they raised families, built an agricultural empire, and fought their enemies with a clear vision of what it meant to be an American, a pioneer, and the backbone of the world's greatest, most powerful, most diverse nation.

Together, they killed the three Mexicans who raped Eula Laws, Jack's granddaughter, in a puddle of filthy water by the dumpster behind the Kentucky Club in Juarez. They hunted them down outside of Juarez and ended their miserable lives, Jack with the powerful 45.70 long rifle he hunted bear with in Montana, and Ali with the same trench knife he used to slash and impale so many Japanese soldiers. They worked and fought together for their entire lives, leading a raid well into their seventies on a Kenyan refugee camp to rescue Amiir Christmas, son of Charlie Christmas, Somali translator and close friend of Jack's great-granddaughter Ademar Zarkan: Army sniper, West Point graduate, and kickass Muslim girl from the high desert of West Texas.

Ademar, who married Jack and Marcie's great-grandson,

Crockett Laws II—Deuce, as they nicknamed him—was the most perfect expression of the union of the two families. The guardian of her runt twin brother, Anil, Ademar was as good with her fists as she was weaving through a barrel race astride a two-thousand-pound quarter horse, taking down a deer from several hundred yards with a .30-30, or drilling a thirty-five-yard kick dead-on through the goalposts on the dusty fields of Texas six-man football for the Dell City Cougars. By the time she was seventeen, the Muslim tomboy with eyes the deep turquoise of Brazilian tourmaline had matured into a woman of exotic beauty. Her lifetime friendship with Deuce, best friend to her older brother, Tamerlane, aged into a love affair as deep as the chasms splitting the soaring Guadalupe Mountains near Dell City. Together, they navigated the most challenging paths: West Point, Iraq, Somalia, Afghanistan, and the war on terrorism. But none more traumatic than the death of Ademar's beloved older brother at the hands of her radicalized twin, Anil, who detonated a suicide vest outside the European Parliament in Brussels while she watched helplessly from a sniper's perch on a nearby building. Family brought her back from the edge of insanity, along with Charlie Christmas and her US Army captain in Somalia, Prometheus Stone: warrior, philosopher, lapsed Jew.

Charlie and Stone stood by Ademar for her first kill, a two-hundred-yard bull's-eye from her M24 sniper rifle into the face of a Somali pirate off the deck of a lurching ship in the Indian Ocean. Ademar and Stone stood by Charlie as he and his family fled Somalia, a journey that took everything from the Somali refugee except for his son, Amiir. They rescued him from a Kenyan refugee camp, helped them settle in Minnesota with thousands of their countrymen, enabled their survival amid the growing threat from America's burgeoning underbelly of white supremacy, and pulled Amiir from the brink of violence as a reluctant ISIS recruit in Syria. By the turn of the century, all of them had settled into *normal* lives in Minnesota and Texas. Charlie rose in the ranks of a local turkey-processing plant in St. Cloud, and Amiir earned a computer science degree from St. Cloud State. Stone, the former hard-hitting Cornell strong safety, traded in his captain's stripes for a rabbi's kittel and settled down in Minneapolis with his Somali wife, Amina, and son, Noah. Ademar and Deuce went back to Dell City and the farm, where they raised their son, Tamerlane Laws, nicknamed T3 after his dead uncle. The dangers of their past seemed to evaporate into distant memories, like mist over a cold lake yielding to a warm late-autumn sun. And they all began to feel *normal*.

Normal, until the Fall.

CHAPTER 3

BEFORE THE FALL

Mornings on the farm in Dell City had not changed much over more than seven decades. The Zarkans hewed to the comforting rituals of Islam as the sun breached the foothills of the Guadalupe Mountains, with one of five daily salahs, prayers dictated by the Muslim faith. Their rituals had remained consistent through the ebbs and flows of national religiosity over the past seventy years—from the mystic trends of the sixties that elevated Eastern gurus to the upper echelons of popular culture alongside the likes of John Lennon; to the pseudo fundamentalism that brought Donald Trump to the White House on a comically hypocritical right-to-life, right-to-execute platform; and to the present day, where the national faith seemed to be a surefire confidence in the artificial intelligence and algorithms that controlled everything. Even the election in 2036 of President Nico Pompador, another hard-right buffoon, didn't faze them or shake their confidence in the power of *la familia* to endure. Year in and year out, the Zarkans greeted the rising sun on their knees murmuring Asr, with the enticing aroma of a country breakfast simmering in the kitchen under the watchful eye of Jack, Crockett, or Deuce Laws. So West Texas, even thirty-six years into the twenty-first century. Humility before God, followed by a plate of huevos rancheros.

Arwen Laws, Ademar's granddaughter and T3's daughter, was only one-quarter Muslim, but she liked the communal intimacy and deep connection to another culture she felt by joining her relatives. Arwen, a redhead due to a long-dormant recessive gene dating back to ancestors in the Levant, didn't necessarily consider herself Muslim, or an adherent to any particular faith. Not yet twelve, she didn't realize it, but Arwen was an animist who could communicate with trees, plants, animals, and most of all her beloved dog, Star, an eighteen-month-old mix of yellow Lab and husky who was equal parts frolicking puppy and ferocious defender of his waiflike ginger master.

Arwen's younger brother fidgeted behind her and tickled her feet, histrionically tumbling back into the kitchen with a mischievous laugh when his sister delivered a gentle back-kick. Morning prayers done, they all took their places around the enormous pecan-wood table in the communal grand room connecting the generous ranch-style homes of the Lawses and the Zarkans. Jack and Ali had searched high and low throughout West Texas for the perfect pecan tree to cut planks for this table that for decades would serve as a symbol of the inviolable bond between them, and spent months sanding and finishing this altar for their families. The twenty-foot table was irregular and round, dark in some places and light in others, a coincidental metaphor for the unlikely yet durable multiethnic union of the Lawses and Zarkans. If there was a religious tablet for the two families, a set of implied commandments brought down from the mountain by Jack and Ali, that table was it. Prometheus Stone conducted a tabletop military exercise there for the rescue of Charlie Christmas and his son, Amiir, from a

Kenyan refugee camp. The wild-as-a-March-hare Eula Laws, Jack and Marcie's only daughter, had lost her virginity there to a blue-eyed cowboy. As many births as deaths had taken place on it, and more than a few fists had pounded it in the heat and friction of a family spat. Arwen, head on a swivel taking in one comment or another about politics, community matters, sports scores, or the weather, was often the last one up from the table. But today she was in a hurry and barely finished her breakfast.

"What's the rush?" Ademar said.

"Quick ride on Boquillas before school," Arwen replied, referring to her five-year-old quarter horse named for a canyon in Big Bend National Park a few hours from Dell City. "Please!"

"All good, baby girl," T3 said. "Check those pivots in the west cantaloupe field while you're at it. Broken sprinkler head, software acting up."

"Affirmative, Dad."

Ademar, who was the closest thing Arwen had to a mother since the untimely death of her own from the latest Covid variant, accompanied her granddaughter to the stable. Ademar was a horse woman to the core, a champion barrel racer in her youth, who, at almost seventy, still rode nearly every day. She had won a legendary Texas cutting horse from her old friend Sam Middleton, former owner of the iconic Four Sixes Ranch, in a game of seven-card stud at the Houston rodeo a few years back. Sam, Marfa low crown low over his eyes, drew to a royal flush during a *casual* hand in the stable one night after the competition. Ademar, three aces down, knew from experience what an old bluffer he was and raised the ante.

"All in," she said. "And both my cutting horses."

Sam chuckled and spat a stream of Copenhagen into the dust at his feet. "Alrighty then, little lady. Figure Metallic Echo is worth those two old nags of yours."

"Call, old timer," and Ademar flipped her cards to reveal the three bullets.

"Jesus, Ademar, didn't figure you for that kind of gambler," Sam sputtered as he conceded his bluff, tilted his cowboy hat back with a finger, and wiped a few brown flecks of snuff from the corner of his mouth.

"Never bluff a bluffer, Sam."

And that's how Ademar came to own one of the most decorated cutting horses in Texas.

Ademar would have liked nothing more than to saddle Echo and accompany Arwen on an early morning ride, but she had other chores in mind.

"Take Echo," Ademar said, and Arwen's green eyes lit up like the lantern on an eastbound train out of the Amtrak station in Alpine. "Can't join you today, honey."

Arwen, a few steps away from the stable where Bo, her usual mount, chuffed and stamped in anticipation of a gallop, stopped dead in her tracks. Wiry with the lean muscles of a West Texas farm girl, Arwen hefted the thirty-pound Billy Cook Western saddle from the rack and ambled over to Echo's stall. Ademar rubbed the soft, prickly hairs on Echo's nose and threw a Green Diamond wool felt saddle pad over the stallion's back. Arwen propped the heavy saddle on her knee and popped it over Echo's back, perfectly situated between his withers and hip. Ademar could have fiddled with it an inch or two, but Arwen would have taken affront to the meddling even though she wouldn't have shown any indignation toward her grandmother. Nor did she chime in as Arwen lowered the saddle straps under Echo's belly, strung the tie through the ring on the girth strap, looped it through the dee, tightened and secured it, then tucked away the excess. Ademar smiled, and Arwen knew it without looking back over her shoulder.

"Good to go, Abuela," said Arwen and, in less than a minute, attached the weathered working bridle from Big Bend Saddlery in Alpine.

Ademar whistled to Star, who was watching it all from a narrow opening between a few hay bales to the side and eyeing a mouse gnawing away on a kernel of corn a few feet away. The dog perked up her ears, stretched with her butt in the air in a position yogis aptly enough refer to as *downward dog*, and ran joyously to Ademar. A cloud of dust puffed up around Star as she put on the brakes and slid the last few feet, tail wagging like a canine metronome, head slightly to the side with that winsome smile only a dog lover loves.

"Take Star and the thirty," said Ademar, sliding the Henry lever-action .30-30 into the scabbard tied to the saddle.

"Yes, ma'am," said Arwen, who, like every woman in the lineage of Lawses and Zarkans, had a way with the long rifle. The petticoat would have to wait a few years.

"You won't take offense if I follow you with the drone?" Ademar asked. "Not worried about you, but your dad wants a look-see at that pivot."

"All good," said Arwen and, with the slightest pressure from her boots on Echo's side, trotted out of the stable with Star charging ahead of them both as the drone hovered overhead like a silent partner in the crisp West Texas morning. Arwen yelled over her shoulder on the way out of the gate. "Text y'all in a bit when I'm there. Gonna ride some first."

Once out of eyesight, Arwen rode like the wind. Her waist-length red hair floated horizontally like a bed of tangled kelp on a wave. She leaned slightly over Echo's neck, their bodies in perfect rhythm. Baryshnikov and Makarova executing a perfect equine ballet. Faster and faster. Star leaped and darted around them, stopping every now and then to sniff at a gopher hole or to dart after a jackrabbit with ears as long as cornstalks. Arwen was living her best life, uninitiated into human guile, free and galloping across the high desert with the two best friends a young girl could hope to have.

Arwen reined in Echo, and the three of them walked through the cantaloupe field. She texted T3, and he lowered the drone close to the suspect sprinkler head on the pivot, which was broken, spewing water even though the sophisticated agro-software told him there was nothing wrong.

"I don't get it," T3 muttered to himself, just as an advertisement for Justin Boots at Allen's on South Congress in Austin popped up on his computer screen, followed by another of a Black rapper hyping Corona beer on a beach in Mexico, then one for some Texas Republican promising to finish the wall of lasers and artificially intelligent automatic weapons along the border to deter migrants. "God damn algorithms."

"Tks. IDK! Ima do it the old way," he texted Arwen and made a mental note to go out to the field later in the day.

"KK," Arwen replied. "West tank for a swim, then home."

Arwen knew the farm like the back of her hand and made a beeline to the tank, a corrugated-steel watering hole as big as a backyard swimming pool in the hoity-toity neighborhoods of Dallas or Houston. Fresh, cold water constantly cycled through it, courtesy of the Bone Spring–Victorio Peak Aquifer that ran like blood through the veins of the farm. And Arwen smiled, always smiled, when she looked at the faded splash of graffiti Ademar and Deuce had painted on the side during their teenage courtship. *Ademar + Deuce.* She imagined them smooching in the tank and thought to herself, *Yuck!* With the innocence of a prepubescent West Texas farm girl, still uninitiated in the ways of the strutting quarterback or the blue-eyed cowboy, Arwen stripped down to her birthday suit and climbed into the tank. Star, with a joyful bark, made it in with a single leap over the four-foot wall of the tank and splashed around snapping at the froth as Arwen lolled on her back. Natural and innocent, Arwen touched herself between the legs and under the arms, wondering nonchalantly when hair might come. Like most young people, Arwen had no idea what came with it. All she knew about that was Cinderella.

They climbed out of the tank, shook a time or two to fling off the big drops, and plopped down on a calico blanket Arwen had laid under a pecan tree next to a pile of syenite boulders. Arwen squeezed into her mouth the green gelatin from a tube of the latest vegan superfood protein goop available at the Two T's grocery store in Dell City. Star wasn't having any of it, preferring the undigested oats in a pile of dung Echo deposited a few yards away. She would have been all over some mayonnaise-slathered B from a BLT, and so would Arwen, but B and mayo didn't keep very well on a warm day in the high desert. Arwen stretched out on the blanket, and Star laid her heavy, damp head in the crook of her best friend's neck. Angels in paradise, they drifted off under the clouds in the shade of a grand pecan tree.

Arwen dreamed often, and in most of those dreams she would communicate with trees, flowers, and animals. Sometimes it was benign, a tree seeming to beckon as it bent in the wind or a butterfly leading the way somewhere. Other times these dreams seemed like a warning of something her young, innocent mind could not fathom. In the age of algorithms and artificial intelligence, she was hard-wired to nature. The foreboding dreams came more frequently the older she grew, and the more radicalized, divided, virused, and climactically chaotic the world became. One night she dreamed of a whale, although she never saw one except online. Thereafter, the whale appeared in almost every dream, always alone, always seeming to search for something in the vast depths of the ocean, and always calling like a sonorous, haunting bagpipe for Arwen's help. At least that's how she interpreted it.

Something brushed against Arwen's cheek. She opened her eyes, and of course, even though Star had been sleeping until that exact moment, Arwen awoke to a dog that seemed to have never slept. They had both been stirred from slumber by a pecan that had dropped from a branch on the tree above them. Arwen heard two sounds: humming from the drone hovering above them, and the unmistakable chatter from the tail of a rattlesnake not more than four feet away and slithering sideways ever closer by the second. T3 had been monitoring the drone feed and would have seen the snake, a Mojave, the deadliest of all rattlers, with neurotoxic venom to paralyze and hemotoxic to bleed. But his feed was stuck on algorithmic-driven advertisement for boots, beer, and the twentieth season of *Yellowstone*.

Arwen knew better than to move. But Star, like most dogs, particularly ranch dogs in West Texas, knew exactly what she had to do. Slowly, with the hair raised on her back, Star lifted up, halfway up with her ears back, her lips curled, and a low, menacing growl deep in her chest. Arwen pictured what might be coming. She had seen such confrontations before, and they always ended in death, either for the snake or the dog. She could see in her mind's eye Star in midair leaping over her. She could hear the rattle on the snake's tail come alive as if it had a life of its own—louder, more frenzied as the deadly reptile raised a few feet from the ground with its head cocked back, ready to strike. She knew Star, at the last minute, would try to twist up and to the right, narrowly avoiding the triangular head and the fully cocked needles of death. And if Star success-fully avoided those fangs, her paws would pin the head of the rattler, eyes cold and unflinching, to the ground and rip off its head. Arwen could imagine with the same clarity the outcome if Star missed, even by just a few inches. She shuddered at the thought of blood oozing from two small puncture wounds on Star's face, the inevitable and immediate swelling, and the slow death in spasms of breathlessness and pain.

In those few milliseconds before the moment of truth, she recalled the words of White Eagle, the Lakota Sioux shaman who had rescued Ademar and Charlie Christmas years ago from white supremacists at the bottom of a slot canyon in the South Dakota Badlands. "We do not fear the serpent. She heals. She transforms. She is a guide to the life force and to the universe's primal energy. Do not fear the serpent. Respect her."

Arwen, the pecan in one hand, felt the connection White Eagle had described to her. She raised her hand slowly in front of Star's face.

"Hold!"

And Star, trembling but obedient, held.

The rattle stopped. And the three of them—snake, dog, girl—seemed joined in a kind of holy trinity to the connectivity of earth. Reptile, beast, and human. The Mojave lowered its body to the ground, and, just as quickly as it had appeared, it disappeared into the rocks. Arwen wondered if this had been another dream.

Back at the house, T3 had no idea what had happened, which was probably better because he couldn't have done anything about it anyway. He rebooted the computer, and the drone flitted aimlessly away until it reconnected.

"Back," he texted Arwen. "Cool?"

"Cool," she texted back and flashed a thumbs-up to the drone.

"Keep this one to ourselves," Arwen said to Star, who understood clearly and simply wagged the tip of her tail in the dust.

Arwen tucked the pecan, the warning from the tree, into the front pocket of her jeans and rode back to the house.

CHAPTER 4

BEFORE THE FALL

US president Nico Pompador was certain another drill for a national emergency was not the best use of his time. He was a West Point graduate and former Army captain with a law degree from Harvard and several elected or appointed federal offices on his résumé, including secretary of defense. He understood the need for preparedness and was mildly alarmed at the recent hack of the National Security Agency's automated parking system by a web of URLs that originated in the Russian Far East and spoofed around Central Europe until it found a way into the underground garage at Fort Meade. The American nuclear arsenal was still under the ultimate command of humans, and not a single missile could be launched without his authorization. Benign systems, like parking, even at the heart of US intelligence, were another matter. Microsoft had been awarded a multimillion contract by the US General Services Administration—the general manager of the government, so to speak—for parking at all federal buildings in and around Washington. Pompador was assured that the glitch in the system, errant code generated by ChatGPT-9, had been fixed and that the digital worm that had wriggled itself across the Atlantic had been isolated and crushed.

"What a great country," Pompador said to the military aide accompanying him on the elevator many floors underneath the East Wing of the White House, where he would participate in his third simulation behind the hardened walls of the Presidential Emergency Operations Center.

"Yes, sir," replied the Army officer, adjusting the handcuff on her left wrist that secured the nuclear *football* and the *biscuit*, a piece of plastic no larger than a credit card that the president would crack open like a crisp biscuit to reveal the ever-changing codes for launching a nuclear strike. "Apologies for disrupting your day, but you know how the military likes to drill."

"How could I forget, Lieutenant?" said Pompador. "West point: drill, drill, drill. Did you know I graduated first in my class?"

"Yes, sir. You mentioned it the last time we went through this drill."

Once the biometric access system had scanned both of their fingerprints and eyeballs, the elevator doors to the PEOC opened to reveal a high-tech command center—a warren of offices, dormitories, and a distinctly unpresidential presidential apartment that could have doubled for a suite at a suburban La Quinta. Hailing from rural Ohio, Pompador was no stranger to suburban motels. The memories of lurid trysts in those darkened rooms with ambitious interns or lusty, plump aides of both genders always gave him a woody if he thought hard enough on it. The tacky furniture, the peeling mini fridge lined with airline bottles of clinking Jack Daniel's bottles, the lingering scent of disinfectant, and those bars of soap wrapped in cheap, crinkly translucent wax paper triggered him in ways no costumes or sex toys in his wife's closet could. Yes, she tried, he often thought, and it was just short of pitiful. Pompador could never complete it with his wife if he couldn't squeeze his eyes closed and imagine himself hunched over a young thing in some cheap motel room. His mind, and his nether regions, began to drift to the memories of those licentious encounters when he glanced at the presidential apartment. Pompador felt a slight tightening in his groin but immediately looked away and started counting backward from one hundred, his surefire remedy for avoiding those distinctly unpresidential triggers.

Pompador knew the drill. It was just the two of them in the main room surrounded by computer screens, communications gear, and large television monitors that could feed real-time images from almost anywhere in the world via a network of military satellites. His aide pulled out a seat for him at the head of the immense, polished wood table in the center of the room. Pompador gripped the edge of the table, eight fingers on top and his thumbs underneath, and leaned back against the leather chair. A man in full. He imagined other presidents whose fingers might have been in this exact position during crises: Roosevelt, Truman, Ike, Kennedy, Carter, his hero Reagan, and all those who came after. The list included Vice President Dick Cheney, one of Pompador's mentors, who stood in for President George W. Bush on 9/11 when W was showing his "compassionate conservative" side reading a book to a classroom full of kids at the Emma Booker Elementary School in Sarasota, Florida. And of course, it also included President Obama when Navy Seals took out Osama bin Laden during a daring nighttime raid in Pakistan. Pompador imagined himself presiding over the hit on America's enemy number one, surrounded by the likes of then secretary of state Hillary Clinton in a tan tweed jacket with one hand cradling her chin, Vice President Joe Biden in shirtsleeves, and National Security Advisor Tom Donilon in the background.

"So, this is where my buddy Dick Cheney sat on 9/11 and where Obama took out bin Laden," Pompador said. "Heavy."

"No, sir," the lieutenant said. "That was actually the Situation Room, a few floors up."

"Whatever, Lieutenant," he said. "You get my meaning."

"I suppose, sir. Shall we start the drill?"

She flipped on the computer screen in front of the president, and the face of an Air Force captain deep in a bunker at North American Aerospace Defense Command headquarters near Colorado Springs flashed on the screen. "Good morning, sir. Shall we begin?"

"Initiating," said the lieutenant in the room with Pompador and unlocked the handcuffs to the nuclear football, then the actual valise, and handed the biscuit to the president.

Pompador felt like God.

As many times as he had held the biscuit, embedded with the power to launch thousands of nuclear warheads and vaporize the world, each time felt like the first. Not even a spine-bending climax in a tawdry suburban motel room could compare. Pompador felt an erection coming on.

"Sir," the lieutenant said.

"What?" replied Pompador somewhat impatiently.

"The codes, sir."

"Yep." He cracked open the biscuit with a sharp snap and read to the captain in Colorado the series of numbers and letters that would unleash the nuclear arsenal.

Just as the simulation software was about to go through the dry run of nuclear annihilation, the president's screen went blank.

"What the fuck," Pompador said.

"Some kind of glitch," the aide said. "Probably that new version of ChatGPT."

"A glitch in this!" the president shouted. "Not my grandson's PlayStation! Not the nuclear weapons system of the United States!"

The lieutenant picked up a red telephone, one just like the Gotham police commissioner would use to contact the caped crusader in the old Batman series from the 1960s, and called the captain in Colorado. At that exact moment, the screen in front of the president, and dozens of others in front of observers for the drill, came alive with a grainy black-and-white video feed from a brightly lit motel room. The president gasped at the images of him strapped to a bed while a young woman in a voluminous pink lace antebellum gown rode him like a bucking stallion while twisting his left nipple into a clamp. A few seconds later, a Guy Fawkes mask overlaid the video. Anonymous, the decentralized international hacktivist collective, still up to its tricks after twenty-five years.

"Good morning, Mr. President," said the muffled voice under the mask of Guy Fawkes, the trademark of Anonymous that resembled the provincial Catholic revolutionary Guido Fawkes, who participated in the infamous Gunpowder Plot of 1605 in England.

"What!" the president sputtered. "Who!"

"This program is brought to you by Anonymous," the masked man said. "We did the NSA parking garage too, with the help of a handy algorithm and a worm in your AI software.

"Enjoy . . . sir. The rest of the world certainly is, courtesy of Twitter."

The mask faded out of the picture, and the video of the domination of the president faded in, with a Twitter feed in the upper right-hand corner blowing up with likes and laughing emojis accumulating by the thousands. It ended in about thirty seconds, revealing something else about the president and his fragile manhood, with an animated blob of white goo splattering all over the video.

"Abort," the lieutenant said, and the simulation ended.

"Very clever," said the president. "Obviously a fake."

The president called his press secretary. "It's a fake. Fake news. Put that out to the press. Use those words, and attribute it to me."

Back in Dell City, Arwen was sitting at the oak table in the dining room examining the unshelled pecan that had saved her life. She was thinking about what might be inside the husk when, at that moment, it opened like a flower to reveal the hard brown endocarp. A white wormlike weevil less than a quarter-inch long wriggled out. She shuddered, not out of any sense of squeamishness but out of a sense of foreboding. It was as if everything in the universe that was not digital, not driven by algorithms, not controlled by artificial intelligence, not owned by Jeff Bezos, Elon Musk, or Mark Zuckerberg, was communicating with her.

The Terra-Algorithm, the antithesis of the digital algorithm that drove everything in the world, began to unfold in Arwen's young mind, as if she peered down a long, dark tunnel that was civilization in its current state to a bright light shining through the terminus of the passageway to something else. The universe, the Terra-Algorithm, Carl Jung's collective unconscious. Images of all the strange interactions she had with trees, flowers, insects, horses, reptiles, and dogs flashed through her mind like photographs cycling through a slide carousel. She was not afraid. Even at twelve, she was not afraid. She was sentient, transformed. Ademar sensed they were more than coincidences when Arwen recounted them, but that's what she called them. Coincidences. Ademar knew better. And now, so did Arwen.

That night Arwen dreamed of the whale, a long dream that ended with her on a beach in some kind of danger and the leviathan impossibly close to the shore, levitating its full one hundred feet into the air. She awoke with the pecan in her hand and Star tucked into her side, bright-eyed and awake, as always. And she knew the whale had a name. 52 Blue.

CHAPTER 5

BEFORE THE FALL

The United States of America had held the line for 244 years. She teetered through wars, protests, political crises, financial ruin, and disease. But she held the line. What began as an idea—an ideal, really—among George Washington, Thomas Jefferson, James Madison, and thirty-six other men who signed the US Constitution on a fall day in Philadelphia had stood for more than two centuries as a living testament for people and nations aspiring to live free.

But in 2020 democracy seemed to have run its course. The line, that thin cordon between freedom and chaos that flutters in the winds of history, snapped. And what rushed in behind it was unspeakable and unfathomable to millions of Americans whose apathetic patriotism had blinded them to the violent radicalism that had seeped into almost every community. The symptoms were clear if anyone had been alert: racism, antisemitism, disenfranchisement, inequality, and injustice. The Oath Keepers, QAnon, and the Proud Boys were the vanguard on the far right—violent white nationalists, armed, organized, with a shocking number of their foot soldiers having served in the military or law enforcement. The far left was a different phenomenon altogether. By 2020, they had finally taken off the gloves after more than a century of benign apathy, equivocation, and "even-handedness" that some equated to complicity. Decentralized groups like Antifa and Anonymous, steeped in the rhetoric of revolutionary thinkers like the American communist and journalist John Reed, were less well armed and organized than the far right and were dismissed by many as nothing more than a bunch of hippies prancing around on a holistic yoga retreat in India or Mexico. But their radicalism ran deep, and their members harbored grievances that ran from Emmett Till to George Floyd and from Abbie Hoffman to Ruth Bader Ginsburg. They were through with the benign pacifism of Mahatma Gandhi and Martin Luther King. They fought in the streets of Portland and in the hidden chat rooms of Discord. They were clever enough not to cross the line like the hard right, which drank the Kool-Aid of Donald Trump and his golems— Stephen Miller, Steve Bannon, and Doug Mastriano, a leader of the white-Christian nationalist movement—and lapped up the dregs of Trumpism from propagandists like Tucker Carlson and Joe Rogan as if it was manna from God.

On January 6, 2021, they not only crossed the line; they snapped it like a dry twig. After that, a *united* states of America seemed like the punchline to a bad joke.

Washington DC Metropolitan Police inspector Robert Glover watched the line stretch to its breaking point, then break.

It began benignly enough with a march on the Capitol to protest what many perceived as a stolen election, and it ended in violence and death, courtesy of the defeated president, who exhorted his acolytes to *stop the steal* by storming the Capitol.

"All of us here today do not want to see our election stolen by radical-left democrats, which is what they're doing, and the fake news media," Trump barked at the crowd gathered in front of the White House. "We will never give up. We will never concede. Our country has had enough, and we will not take it anymore."

Inspector Glover, who was in charge of crowd control, stood bravely with his forces behind the actual line, a network of flimsy bicycle racks that had never been breached in the face of protest. But they fell like dominoes as the hard-right throngs—radicalized, drunk with Trumpism and wielding bear spray, truncheons, and in some cases handguns—surged onto the west front of the Capitol. He heard their battle cries. "The patriots are the only ones who give a fuck." . . . "Push, push, push." . . . "Get their helmets off." And finally, at 2:28 p.m., like Davy Crockett at the Alamo, Glover had to concede that the line, the actual line and the metaphorical line between democracy and chaos, had broken.

"We've been flanked," he yelled into his walkie-talkie. "We've lost the line."

CHAPTER 6

BEFORE THE FALL

Arwen was of an age at which she was troubled by the state of the world. The high desert of West Texas was remote, but not walled off from the rest of the planet. The impact of climate change was everywhere—the packs of feral hogs, the water shortages, extreme heat, and the outbreaks of respiratory viruses that had transformed education and any semblance of public life into a game of chance, a flip of the coin. Heads, you're a denier, even unto your death bed; tails, you're a masked pariah.

Arwen's main source of straight news in West Texas was Marfa Public Radio, an NPR affiliate, one of the last remaining balanced news organizations. The news wasn't any more palatable, but at least those who still listened knew they could trust it. Morning Edition was the background chatter to the foreground chatter at every family breakfast. Arwen often tuned out the latter and listened intently to reports of global tensions mounting: skirmishes along the demilitarized zone between the Koreas; last-ditch summits over Taiwan; NATO expansion; nuclear tensions between the United States, Russia, and China; and the near-daily terrorist bombings everywhere, including the United States. Most disturbing of all, the Web had outgrown its architecture, and maverick algorithms, operating independently of humans, were doing a lot more than pushing ads for shoes or dishwashers. The US Department of Homeland Security had created an entire division to chase the algorithms as if they were a modern-day cyber mafia with AI-driven capos executing their bidding. Penetrating blockchains was child's play, and the crypto markets, so recently considered the Holy Grail of modern finance, teetered on the brink of collapse due to renegade artificial intelligence. The Saudi government had lost control of its ability to regulate oil flows, still critical for the world economy in the absence of significant wind or solar production, which the carbon lobby in states like Texas and West Virginia had successfully stalled at every legislative turn. The propaganda arms of almost every government tried to hide and spin, but the public was not fooled anymore. Their lame attempts seemed more like duck and cover.

Arwen imagined how it must have been decades ago for Ademar and her husband, Crockett Laws, with not much more to worry about than high school football games, rodeo, and the prom. Arwen had begun the blossoming from girl to woman and had once overheard her grandparents talking about the night after their senior prom, when Ademar and Crockett had lain together under saddle blankets in the back of a pickup truck at the base of the Guadalupe Mountains. What stuck with her was the image of the pickup's lights shimmering like diamonds in the eyes of deer bedded down for the night. Romance was a fairy tale for a young girl, like shimmering diamonds on a pitch-black high desert night in Far West Texas. There were still shimmering diamonds of hope for Arwen, even as the rest of the world melted like a sandcastle under a rising tide.

No Marfa Public Radio this morning. Arwen had awakened before dawn to accompany her father, Tamerlane Laws III, T3, on an overnight fishing trip in Big Bend National Park, four hours southeast on Interstate 90, then dead south on 118. To her great delight, they would be accompanied by the legendary warrior rabbi Prometheus Stone and his son, Noah, who were visiting from Minneapolis.

Stone—Cap, as they called him—was Ademar's captain during the failed US intervention in Somalia decades ago, and their friendship had endured dramas both large and small. Stone, a standout defensive back at Cornell and four-time champion in the annual intramural boxing tournament whose nickname as a pugilist was the Yom Kippur Clipper, had enlisted in the Army after college, much to his parents' chagrin. They had expected him to enter yeshiva and graduate a rabbi like three previous generations of Stone patriarchs. He joined the rabbinate in Minneapolis after twenty years as an Army Ranger, an unlikely rabbi in faded jeans and black T-shirt, biceps still knotted and stomach tight like a man a third his age. Stone's hair was flecked with gray, but he still had much of it. His long-winded stories, laced with philosophy and ironic humor, delighted anyone close enough to hear them, especially Arwen. Stone had married Amina, a Somali American nearly half his age, and their son, Noah, was like a big brother to Arwen. He taught her all about ice hockey on frequent visits to Minnesota, and she had tutored him on the finer points of horsemanship and long rifles in Dell City. Cap—the angling rabbi, as T3 dubbed him for this trip—had honed his fly-fishing skills on the St. Croix River in Minnesota, and he would impart the finer points of that sweet science to all of them during this trip to Big Bend.

They had loaded the truck well before dawn with the inflatable raft, fly rods, camping gear, and a cooler full of tortilla-wrapped salpicon, eggs, fruit, Gatorade, and Lone

Star. Despite Islam's prohibition on alcohol, T3 figured Allah would make an exception for a few longnecks on a fishing trip with the rabbi. What an unlikely pair, the Muslim farmer and the Jewish warrior who knew his way around the Torah just as well as an M24. How could Allah, or anyone else, object? Star fidgeted at the door as they packed, anxious that they might forget her because she hadn't seen or smelled any dog food going into the truck. Arwen had forgotten all about Star in the drowsy ritual of preparations for a pre-dawn fishing trip and couldn't understand why she was frozen at the door to the house.

"Forgot something, baby girl," said Ademar, standing in the doorway with a bag of kibble.

"Oh yeah," Arwen mumbled from the back seat of the truck and hopped out to retrieve it. Star leaped into the bed of the truck before Arwen had taken a step.

Arwen was particularly excited at the prospect of seeing the emergence of the seventeen-year cicada, which was expected at this exact time. Scientists and mystics alike saw their appearance, or absence, as an important barometer for the true state of the climate, and the future of the world. Even though the periodic cicadas had been about eight inches underground for seventeen years, they were not immune to the rising carbon levels and global warming. There were certainly cicadas in Big Bend National Park, but the seventeen-year variety were largely a phenomenon of the northeast United States. It would be an anomaly of nature should they suddenly claw their way to the surface in the high desert of West Texas, and a sign that not even the most ardent climate denier could ignore.

Arwen could not stop chattering about the cicadas on the 260-mile drive to Big Bend National Park and barely ate her green-chili cheeseburger or drank her coke at Mom's Kitchen in Van Horn.

"Cap, you paying attention?" Arwen said.

"Gotta take a leak," he replied.

"Well, then, I'll wait until you're back. This is the important part."

She resumed the tutorial once Stone returned to polish off his grilled cheese and bacon. Just like T3, who figured there was a time and place Allah might look the other way on a cold one, Stone figured his deity would turn a blind eye on a little pork, particularly drowning in the good old American cheese dripping down the crust of white bread at Mom's.

"The cicadas are homopterans," Arwen said proudly, citing a report she'd done on them that year for her science class. "That means they are one of thirty-two thousand species of sucking insects, most of them with transparent wings like the cicada.

"Seventeen years ago, after just over a month of life, the last batch bred and stuck its eggs underground. You know what they did down there for seventeen years?"

"Hibernated?" Noah answered.

"No, they don't hibernate, contrary to what most folks think," Arwen replied. "The nymphs, that's what they're called at this stage, squirm around feeding on tree sap. Tree sap! Seventeen years eating the same thing for breakfast, lunch, and dinner. How would you like that, Cap?"

"Can't say that I would," he replied. "MREs aren't much better."

"Well, they're insects, and they don't care. They don't really even have a brain, at least not like us. And they just squirm around for seventeen years sucking tree sap. But, once the temperature of the dirt around them hits the mid-sixties, voilà. They pop up for a month or so, fly around mating, at least the ones lucky enough not to be eaten by dogs or crushed by a car or whatever, and bury their eggs underground. Seventeen years later, it happens all over again. That's the way it's always been, even going back to bible times."

"And why is that important, baby girl?" T3 asked.

"Dad, I'm almost a teenager! Puh-leaze stop calling me baby girl.

"It's important cuz they may come up here. That would prove the climate is changing, changing things that have been happening forever. And scientists could analyze our air and water by testing the cicadas. Remember, they've been drinking tree sap for seventeen years. And the trees live on air and water. I feel like the trees could be sending us a message. And the cicadas are the messengers. Interesting, huh?"

She elbowed Noah in the ribs. "There will be a quiz later, Mr. Warsame."

They arrived midafternoon at Lajitas, the put-in for floating and fishing trips through Santa Elena Canyon, and were on the water in an hour. As if Arwen had passed the environment torch to her dad, T3 provided some background on the history of the luxe Lajitas Golf Resort and Spa nestled between the national and state parks.

"What the F," he said, pointing to fairways as green as Pebble Beach or Augusta. "Imagine how much water that takes!"

"One of the Microsoft founders built it, spent millions. Few years back, sold it to a guy named Kelcy Warren, full-on Texas douchebag."

"What's a douchebag?" Arwen asked, and Noah exploded in laughter.

"Um," said T3, not sure how far along Ademar was with that particular aspect of Arwen's education. "It's an expression for someone who's a jerk, someone who buys a statue of Robert E. Lee in Dallas and relocates it on his golf course in West Texas.

"Anyway, Warren is part owner of an outfit called Texas Energy Partners—oil and gas fat cats who built a one-hundred-dred-and-forty-three-mile propane pipeline into Mexico across the Big Bend. His Mexican partner is a dude named

Carlos Slim. Carlos Slim! Can't make that shit up. A lot of ranchers and Indigenous folks went ballistic. Mexicans produce a ton of propane and don't need it. Propane at one thousand four hundred pounds per square inch in an above-ground forty-two-inch pipe cutting through our Big Bend. Recipe for disaster! Lightnin' strikes, javelina, coyotes, tarnaydahs, rust, vandals. And they had to clear a big swath along those one hundred and forty-three miles to make a path for the pipes. Remember, Arwen? We saw that a few months ago near Shafter on our way to the El Super in Ojinaga. Looks like some scalped settler after a run-in with Comanches on the Llano Estacado.

"Building that thing was a case study in good old Texas wheeling and dealing, supposedly even included the services of some teenage hookers as bribes."

"What's a hooker?" Arwen asked.

"Um," T3 stammered. "Ask Abuela about that when you ask her about douchebags.

"Anyway, the Mexicans didn't want it, but Slim and Warren never bothered to take it apart or figure out some way to siphon out the gas that's in there. They were so confident in their prostitutes and connections that they built it and gassed it up without any guarantee of approval. Only customer now is a chili-roasting outfit in Presidio."

"Douchebags!" Arwen exclaimed, her new favorite expression.

At that time of day in Big Bend, the last few hours of sun danced on the canyon walls and bounced off the water, conjuring a work of art no human could re-create, although thousands of artists had tried and, mostly, fell short. But that didn't prevent every would-be gallery in Terlingua, the ghost town just outside the entrance to the national park, and owners like Bill Ivey at local hang-outs like the Starlight, from festooning their walls with sketches, watercolors, and oils of the canyon's magical pallet during the late afternoon. To have an authentic Kelly Pruitt painting hanging above your two-story flagstone fireplace in Houston or Dallas was like a Boy Scout merit badge proving you'd passed some kind of ritual test in the Big Bend.

T3 perched on the pontoon at the back of the Avon whitewater raft with a long paddle to keep the raft near Entrance Camp and well above Rockslide, one of the only consequential rapids on the Rio Grande flowing through Santa Elena Canyon. Water flows through dams on the Rio Conchos River coming out of the mountains in northern Mexico could be erratic and dangerous since the authorities south of the border gave up trying to patch software that had been overtaken by machine-educated software that seemed to have a mind of its own. Even more so since a band of eco-raiders and Mexican farmers had blown up a few of the dams to protest the government's callous disregard for the needs of Indigenous agriculture. The Rio Conchos fed the Rio Grande, and surges in water flow could suddenly trap a raft against a boulder, while drops could strand paddlers for days at the base of the soaring rock walls.

"We're good today," said T3, who had checked the water flow an hour ago. "Four hundred CFS."

"*Inshallah*," Stone said, using the Muslim expression for *God willing*. "Arwen, Noah, get your butts up here for a lesson with the lord of the flies."

Trout were unheard of in the Rio Grande, although that might have changed with the shifting climate and unregulated water flow from the mountains. Most anglers chose to drift-fish with a rod and reel for flathead catfish, chub, and gizzard shad. Kids on the Mexican side would make their way into the canyon to fish with makeshift poles fashioned from river cane that grew on the banks and the ubiquitous plastic bobbers that would submerge under the power of a strike.

"Cats, chub, and shad like to feed along the bottom," Stone said as Arwen and Noah crouched around him when he pulled a small fly case from his vest side pocket. "But they aren't immune, no fish is immune, to the Cap special."

Cap put together a drop-shot rig, an eight-inch run of medium tippet weighted with a pea-sized chunk of lead to pull a wet fly to the bottom of the riverbed, where it would bounce around like a struggling insect. He attached it together with two triple surgeon's knots, one to secure the tippet on the fishing line and another to attach the fly to the end of the tippet. Noah and Arwen each had an Orvis Helios, full length and whippy for the long, mostly unobstructed casts deployed on the Rio Grande.

"Let's do it," said Stone, handing the rods to Arwen and Noah. "Arwen on the bow, that's the front, and Noah on the stern.

"Ten and two, ten and two, ten and two, like the hands of a clock. Makes it look like the bug is flying back and forth above the water. Let it sit for a second on the surface, then sink. Lift the rod every now and then so it looks like the bug is coming up and skipping along the surface. Keep the line tight. Strip it in so it goes taut on a strike."

They were fast learners, and within minutes Arwen had hooked a catfish.

"Got one," Arwen yelled as the line went straight and the rod bent to a sweeping arc.

"Big one," Stone said. "Let him run or he'll snap that line."

T3 maneuvered the raft to shallow water so Arwen could bring the fish close enough to the shore for Stone to scoop it with the net. After ten minutes, she pulled back on the rod to take in a chunk of line. The catfish jumped several feet above the water, a magnificent specimen at the peak of his life twisting and turning in midair to free the hook. Arwen could feel the life force of the fish flow up the line and down the pole into her body. Arwen shivered, and an image of the whale, the leviathan in her dreams, flashed through her mind. Arwen worked it and worked it until the cat surrendered to fatigue and drifted into Stone's net. He crouched on the bottom of the raft and leaned over the pontoon to gingerly pull the line and the fish from the net. Arwen stood over him, excited, sweaty, and sad, especially when Stone stuck his thumb in the gills and handed it to her to pull out the hook. The cat's gills struggled for oxygen, and its mouth tore slightly when Arwen dislodged the barb. The fish shuddered, and a drop of blood trickled down its mouth. Arwen had bagged her share of game: deer, whitewing dove, quail, jackrabbit, but this felt different. They all died at a distance, almost inanimate, not attached to her flailing and squirming as if they knew life was seeping from them every second. And she could not shake the image of the whale, who had a name now: 52 Blue.

"Good eating tonight," Stone said. "Hope we remembered the flour, the cast-iron pan."

"Letting him go," Arwen said, with a touch of uncharacteristic petulance, and before anyone could object, she lowered the catfish into the water and held him gently as he aerated his gills and swam away with one powerful thrust.

Silence settled over the raft. The only sound was the rushing of water around the boulders and the chattering of river cane along the bank as the dry West Texas wind funneled through the narrow canyon walls.

"Anything that fights so hard against death deserves to live," Arwen said. "Not end up in pieces sputtering in butter at the bottom of a pan."

"That's right, baby girl," T3 said.

Noah and Arwen caught plenty of fish before they drifted ashore at Entrance Camp, where Santa Elena Canyon officially began and where they would spend the night. They released them all. But nobody would go hungry feasting on the salpicon, charcoaled flank steak marinated overnight with jalapenos and other vegetables, all wrapped in a large tortilla with small squares of asadero cheese. Or thirsty.

This particular juncture of the Rio Grande was a crossing point for undocumented Latin American migrants. They were mostly mothers and children whose husbands had been coerced into the narco life under death threats against their families. Their sons were often slaughtered in broad daylight, their mutilated corpses left hanging from bridges to twist in the wind. The gangs passed their young girls around like sex toys and discarded them in city dumps or shallow graves with a bullet in their heads when the novelty and freshness wore off. The families knew they were next, only a matter of time, and they fled. Desperate mothers in communities like San Pedro Azul in Honduras or Barrio Azteca in Juarez, with daughters they hoped to save from the basest depravities and sons from the narco life and the narco death. They exhausted a lifetime of savings on coyotes, mercenary guides who promised to lead them to *El Norte* and frequently left them in the desert to die of hunger, dehydration, or snakebite. And if they were lucky enough to make it across the river or past the AI-driven guns along the virtual wall, most of the migrants ended up caged in detention camps like dogs in a West Texas kill shelter. 2020 or 2035. Same same.

Star finished his bowl of kibble in record time and strayed from camp to sniff along the riverbank at the detritus migrants left behind before they swam across the Rio Grande: backpacks, Converse high-tops, diapers, toys, Tupperware containers, and the like. He trotted back to camp with what was clearly a human jawbone, dry and cracked from weeks in the harsh desert sun, and dropped it at Arwen's feet. No animal she knew of ever had a silver filling in its back molar. Stone, who'd seen plenty of sunbaked remains in the wake of desert battles from Iraq to Somalia, knew exactly what Star had deposited next to the Chaco on Arwen's left foot.

"What's that?" Arwen asked, although she knew.

"A jaw," Stone replied.

"From what?"

"Human."

"Some caveman or something?"

"No, cavemen don't go to the dentist," Stone said, turning it over to show Arwen the silver fillings.

Silence. Not a word. The only sounds were the crackling of the small fire, the whispering of water over rocks, and the murmur of a spring wind through the green leaves of cottonwood trees. Arwen wrung her hands, then stuck them under her legs, nervous, awkward, disturbed. "Is it . . . was it a child?" Arwen asked.

Stone had been in this type of situation many times with young soldiers after their first battle, after their first kill, and had a feel for what to say.

"It's a hard lesson for someone so young," said Stone, directing his remarks to Arwen and Noah. "No take backs, like with that catfish you released. Permanent. Forever."

"What about Heaven?" Arwen asked.

"Or Hell," Stone said. "Nobody knows. Can't come back to tell anyone. But I think there's something else besides these body bags we walk around in, something after we leave them behind.

"It's a testament in a way, that jawbone. Probably someone chasing a new life away from danger over there," said Stone, motioning across the river to Mexico. He muttered under his breath to T3 on the other side of the small fire, "If they only knew what it was like now in these United States. United . . . Bullshit."

Silent as the mountain lion for which he was named, Mawiya stepped into the light of the fire. Arwen's and Noah's eyes almost popped out of their heads. Stone reached for the Ka-Bar commando knife that he carried every day in the Army and wore concealed in an ankle holster when he visited inmates at Stillwater prison in rural Minnesota. T3, a formidable linebacker at UTEP like his father and grandfather, tensed as if he was about to blitz from the edge. Star, hackles raised and growling, inched forward. But there was something about this thin bronze man in a serape shirt, jogging shorts, and thin sandals that seemed anything but threatening. Mawiya, *mountain lion* in the ancient Uto-Aztecan language of the Indigenous Raramuri tribe that lived an agrarian life across the border in the Mexican state of Chihuahua, flashed a big white smile and laughed.

"*Lo siento, amigos*," he said, touching fingertips with each of them in the traditional Raramuri greeting symbolizing respect, freedom, and sovereignty. "Sorry, didn't mean to startle you. I was looking for someone who left us a few weeks ago. Tracked them eighty miles to that field over there. I hope she didn't end up like that jawbone at your feet."

"How did you get here?" Arwen asked.

"Ran," said Mawiya, whose tribe, sometimes known as the Tarahumara, was renowned for their seeming superhuman ability to run hundreds of miles through the sweltering desert. "We run a lot. Cheaper than gas."

Stone laughed. "I'll say. Have a seat. Cold beer?"

"*Gracias, agua, por favor.*"

"I'll get it," said Arwen, pushing her long red hair out of her eyes and passing a Camelback to Mawiya.

"*Gracias*, Sehta," said Mawiya, using the Raramuri word for *red*. "I'll call you Sehta—Red."

"I like that," she said.

They welcomed Mawiya into their circle, offering food and campsite banter for several hours—the hospitality of one wanderer to another amid the darkness of a desert night.

"You're welcome to stay the night," Stone said.

"*Gracias*, I'll take you up on that," Mawiya said. "I'll run back in the morning. Hard to run at night. Can't see the cactus and the rattlesnakes."

"Sorry," T3 said. "We don't have an extra tent."

"*Sin problema*," Mawiya said.

"Good night, Mawiya," Arwen said as she climbed in the tent she shared with Noah.

"Good night, Sehta," Mawiya replied, curling up by the fire like a cat, or a mountain lion, and wrapping his serape around himself like a blanket. "Good dreams."

Noah was sawing logs a few minutes after his head hit the lifejacket he used for a pillow, but Arwen lay awake for several hours trying to make sense of the kaleidoscope of thoughts and emotions elicited by this day. Despite her age, Arwen processed like someone far older. She thought to herself, Was there a thread that ran through it all that day: the river, the jawbone, the mysterious native running man? She listened to Noah's rhythmic breathing in the sleeping bag next to her. She envied him his sleep. She was tired, but, like an adult with adult concerns, sleep eluded her. Jawbone. Mawiya. It all swirled and swirled in her mind, like a raft trapped in an eddy on a turbulent river. Round and round in the vortex, unable to free itself at the apex of each revolution despite the desperate paddling of its crew. Arwen's last thought before sleep overtook her was of Ademar, her beloved *abuela*, and the whale, 52 Blue, sentient and alone in the deep blue sea, humming and clicking at fifty-two hertz in search of her mate.

But Arwen didn't dream of the whale this night. She dreamed of the cicadas, the seventeen-year cicadas, nourished by tree sap and wriggling their way the last few inches to the light. In her dream, she was standing by a cottonwood tree surrounded by hundreds of tiny mounds of earth under which cicadas were popping up, green, moist, with translucent wings straining to take them aloft after seventeen years of imagining what it might be like to fly. Flight. Freedom. In her dream, Mawiya appeared far away in the distance, loping toward her in perfect strides worthy of the most adept marathon runner. It was as if he was coming to rescue her—from what, she could not see. Certainly not the cicadas, which took to the air one by one and murmurated gleefully like schoolchildren set free into the playground after a morning of math and English. A strong wind swept the swarm of cicadas away from her, and, as Mawiya strode to within a few feet, an older woman, but not Ademar, grabbed her from behind. Arwen couldn't breathe, couldn't move.

She awoke in a cold sweat at dawn, with the dream fresh in her mind. Perhaps it meant the cicadas would come out of their holes this morning, a sign that nature, the earth, was healing itself. She unzipped her tent and poked her head out. Mawiya was crouched over a tiny furrow next to a tree near the water. A few grains of earth were being pushed to the surface by some kind of subterranean miner. Arwen was transfixed. Something began to emerge, inch by inch. Arwen and Mawiya could see it was a cicada, for sure a cicada. But it was black, jet black like a lump of charcoal, with wings of black crust glued impossibly tight to its desiccated body. Mawiya plucked the cicada from the ground and held it in his open palm. Arwen held her breath. The cicada stopped moving. Dead. Arwen, so full of a child's hope, felt as if something in her had died as well. She would never forget, never allow herself to forget, that image: the mythic Raramuri, the bronze running man in the serape and running shorts, holding the dead cicada in his open palm like a shattered mother cradling a stillborn infant. Was it the loss of innocence, or the loss of hope?

Neither Arwen nor Mawiya mentioned it at breakfast. They had shared something that could not be articulated, that had no words, that could not be shared with anyone else. This was their bond, and both of them had a feeling that they would share more, good or bad, in the future. Mawiya thanked them all after breakfast and jogged a few hundred feet to the top of the riverbank. He stopped, turned, and jogged back to Stone and T3. Mawiya placed his right hand just above his heart three times, a traditional thanks to a host or shaman, for each of the three souls Raramuri believed a man possessed. Mawiya held his hand out to Arwen, and, rather than touching just the tip of her finger, pressed his entire finger against hers, signifying deep appreciation. But he was careful not to squeeze her entire hand, tantamount to a marriage proposal.

"You are my friend, Sehta," he said. "You are always welcome in my home."

Arwen watched him jog away until he was one with the horizon, a tiny stick figure receding into the east, into the sun. When she returned to her tent, she found a bracelet, the one Mawiya had worn on his left wrist—eight polished one-inch chunks of smooth, impossibly blue turquoise exquisitely crafted into nearly perfect ovals. Arwen would wear it for as long as she lived.

CHAPTER 7

BEFORE THE FALL

Nico Pompador was back in the saddle. Pete Buttigieg had defeated him fair and square in 2032. Slightly less than half the nation was incensed that a gay man was elected president, and convinced that his victory had been engineered by some combination of the liberal elite: Hollywood, the *New York Times*, the Jews, Black Lives Matter, and Venezuela. The other half were relieved that the US system of elections and democracy had survived, although barely. Pompador ran again in 2036 and won by a narrow margin after his digital guru hacked into the election system and inserted a Trojan Horse that made every vote for him count as two and deleted every other vote from an African American. Violent protesters of every political stripe poured into the streets, a last-ditch effort to salvage democracy, but Pompador crushed them under the bootheels of National Guard troops he knew would uphold their end of a sacred oath to follow the commander in chief. His first order of business was to seize and destroy all the voting machines and ballots; to declare martial law; to detain Buttigieg; to shutter the *New York Times, Washington Post, Wall*

Street Journal, and CNN; and to replace his personal Secret Service detail with paramilitary units composed of Proud Boys and Oath Keepers, some of them veterans of the January 6 Capitol riot. Pompador wore a massive Desert Eagle .50 cal—the *big boy,* as he called it—on his right hip in a leather cowboy holster embossed with an American flag and *America Is Great!* He wore it at his inauguration, surrounded by a security detail that looked more like a band of Hells Angels guarding a Rolling Stones concert than the discreet, well-dressed, and shaved Secret Service details of past presidents.

Chief of Staff Stephen Diller, a weaselly former Trump advisor who had been lurking in cyberspace for years fomenting conspiracy theories and retweeting racist tropes, walked into the Oval Office a few weeks after Pompador's election to make sure the president was not late for his first full-on intelligence briefing.

"Time for the briefing, Mr. President," hissed Diller, who bore a striking resemblance to Gríma Wormtongue, chief counselor to King Théoden in Lord of the Rings.

"Roger that," Pompador said. "By the way, Stephen, what did we do with Buttigieg?"

"House arrest for now, sir."

"I really think he should be with those dunecoons at Gitmo," said Pompador, referring to the US military prison for suspected terrorists near Guantanamo Bay in Cuba.

"Perfect," said Diller, rubbing his hands together as if he was massaging Vaseline into them. "Charges?"

"Oh yeah, we need that, don't we?"

"Not really. At Gitmo, he's considered a prisoner of war. We can dispense with habeas corpus and all that other constitutional crap."

"Charge him with sedition," Pompador said. "And arrest Chasten—wife, husband, butthole buddy, whatever. Who's pitching and who's catching? Put them in adjacent cells so

Buttigieg can stick his dick through the bars and Chasten can suck him off."

"Seriously?" Diller asked.

"Humanitarian gesture," said Pompador. "Don't want to violate his human rights."

The two of them laughed uproariously and exchanged high fives.

"You've got a photo op on the way to the briefing, sir," Diller said. "Stop off at the makeup room on our way."

Pompador smiled, and only Diller knew why. Pompador swung both ways, and he had taken a shine to Tony Fernandez, the White House stylist. Pompador was hard before he even sat down in the makeup chair.

"Give us a minute, Stephen."

"Yes, sir," Diller said as he closed the door quietly behind him.

Tony leaned over Pompador to apply some brightening powder under his eyes. Pompador had unzipped his fly and flopped his manhood out under the apron Tony had wrapped around him to prevent any soiling of the president's white shirt. He grabbed Tony's ass and pushed his head under the apron. "How about a little attention for the general's helmet." The stylist hated every minute of it, longed for the decency of Buttigieg, but wasn't about to forfeit a $90,000-a-year gig over a blow job. Pompador came in less than thirty seconds, nearly ripping off the ears of the stylist, who spat the president's wad into the sink.

"Good boy," said Pompador, flipping a $5 bill on the floor. "The president doesn't need any stains on his trousers."

Pompador faced a bank of photographers in the White House Rose Garden. Diller hovered solicitously just behind his left shoulder and feigned self-important indifference by thumbing through papers in a leather folder he had stamped with *Top Secret* for everyone to see. The president turned slightly to the left and adjusted his coat to be sure the massive gas-operated semi-automatic Desert Eagle peeked out on every photograph. The chief White House correspondent for the Associated Press, the only reporter allowed at photo ops, shouted a question about alleged ballot improprieties.

"Tsk, tsk," said Diller, nodding at one of the Oath Keepers, who grabbed the woman from the AP by the lanyard around her neck, from which dangled White House credentials, and dragged her away. "You know the rules."

She continued to ask the question, but the thug twisted the lanyard so all that came out was a wheezy squeak.

The photo op was over in a matter of minutes, and Pompador followed Diller to the secure Situation Room, the informal name for the John F. Kennedy Conference Room in the White House basement, five thousand square feet of computers, telephones, and monitors reserved for the most sensitive consultations.

The director of central intelligence, the director of the National Security Agency, and the secretaries of defense, state, homeland security, and the treasury stood up as soon as Pompador entered the room and didn't sit back down until he sat at the large, elliptical mahogany table gifted in 1970 by then president Richard Nixon.

"Where do we start?" Pompador said.

"At the beginning, sir," the director of national intelligence said. "And it's not good.

"We'll start on the domestic situation."

Department of Homeland Security director Thomas Frank clicked a remote control, and a ninety-six-inch flat screen on the wall came alive with a satellite image of the Pacific Northwest, from Seattle, Washington, to Cape Mendocino, California. A green line connecting the major cities had been superimposed along the coast, with tags for smaller towns like Portland, Eugene, and Klamath Falls. An orange line labeled

Cascadia Subduction Zone, where the Juan de Fuca and North American tectonic plates met, was drawn just off the coast parallel to the green line on land.

"What am I looking at?" Pompador asked.

"Hell," said Frank as he clicked on another monitor with live drone footage from all of the towns indicated on the satellite image.

"Just looks like ocean to me," Pompador said.

"That's because it is, now," Frank said. "There was a megathrust event twelve hours ago."

"A what?" Pompador said.

"A 9.0 earthquake caused by a sudden drop in the two plates, which triggered a one-hundred-foot tsunami wave that washed over the entire Pacific Northwest. Most of it is gone, thousands killed."

"What's that?" asked Pompador, pointing to a drone feed from Eugene that showed what looked like the platforms atop fire towers with a few adults and dozens of children standing on it.

"The lucky ones," Frank said. "Some of these towers were built near schools in anticipation of just this type of disaster. The Air National Guard is staging the largest evacuation in its history."

"Bigger than Katrina?" Pompador questioned.

Frank suppressed a laugh. "With all due respect, Mr. President, this makes Katrina look like a routine rescue of a struggling kid at a community swimming pool."

"Why the fuck wasn't I informed?" Pompador bellowed. "Why wasn't it in the media?"

"You asked not to be disturbed last night," said Chief of Staff Diller, omitting the part about who the president was with. "And we blacked out all the media, even social media: Twitter, Reddit, YouTube, and the others. But that won't last long."

"What do you suggest?" Pompador, turning to Frank, asked.

"I suggest you keep listening," Frank said. "There's more. A lot more.

"Midland and Odessa are gone too. Heart of the domestic oil industry. Gas stations are under siege. Gunfights for the last drops."

"No way that wave hit West Texas," Pompador said.

"Hydraulic fracking, sir," said Frank as another monitor flashed on a huge hole where Midland and Odessa, pride of the Texas carbon elite, once stood. "Remember when I briefed you several months ago on increased seismic activity in West Texas?"

"Vaguely," Pompador said.

"Not to say I told you so, but I warned that all those small tremors might lead to disastrous consequences. What you're looking at is a disastrous consequence."

"Diller!"

"What can I say, sir?" Diller sputtered. "Last night. Do not disturb."

"Moving on, sir," Director of Central Intelligence Raj Chowdhury said. "To the international side."

Secretary of Defense Matt "Ironhead" Eisenhower, a former US Marine general and direct descendant of Ike, clicked his remote, and the monitors went dark for a moment. Another click and a satellite image of North and South Korea appeared on one of the screens. The others came alive with drone feeds from the Korean Peninsula and the demilitarized zone between North and South at the thirty-eighth parallel, where indistinguishable masses of men engaged in frantic hand-to-hand combat. Seoul, the capital of South Korea, looked like Hiroshima the day after the United States dropped the atomic bomb that ended World War II. One screen was all tiles of US military installations in South

Korea, with maimed and gasping soldiers stumbling like zombies amid the debris.

"We have thirty thousand personnel in South Korea," Eisenhower said. "They will all be dead in a matter of hours, along with hundreds of thousands of civilians on the Korean Peninsula."

"What?" Pompador muttered. "Give me a cigarette."

"You don't smoke," Diller said.

"I do now."

"We're not quite sure how it started, but we're piecing it together," Eisenhower said. "It all started with a mistake. South Korean forces detected a missile from the North last night headed for Seoul, and the air defense system we sold them, the one coded almost entirely by ChatGPT, shot it down. South Korean F-16s scrambled toward the North, and Pyongyang, the Dear Leader, thought it was the vanguard of an invasion. He launched everything they had, thousands of ballistic missiles. Sarin. Anthrax. Smallpox. Conventional."

"Nukes?" Pompador asked.

"Yes, sir," Eisenhower said. "The radiation, the chemicals, the diseases will spread throughout East Asia and beyond within a few hours."

"We estimate deaths in the millions," Director of National Intelligence Chowdhury said.

"What about the Russians and the Chinese?" Pompador asked.

"Both on high alert. They aren't picking up the phone," Eisenhower said. "Neither are we. Waiting to hear from you. But we're detecting massive movements of military, air, and naval assets."

"Russia seems to be preparing for an invasion of Poland and Romania, possibly Latvia, Lithuania, and Estonia," Chowdhury said. "NATO allies. Moscow has also shut the gas pipeline to Europe.

"And China has encircled Taiwan with nuclear-armed submarines. Chinese commandos seized the Samsung and TSMC microprocessor production facilities a few hours ago. In some ways that may be the most alarming development. Those two companies are pretty much the only ones in the world that produce eight-nanometer chips. We use them, and we'd be crippled if the supply was cut off. You can say good-bye to anything that relies on artificial intelligence, machine learning, or algorithms. Pretty much the heart of everything."

"Is this when I order DEFCON one?" Pompador asked sheepishly, referring to the highest level of national defense.

"I'd say so, sir," Eisenhower responded while everyone in the room nodded.

"Okay," said Pompador, dropping one hand to rest on his pistol as if he was preparing for a gunfight. "DEFCON one! I've always wanted to do that.

"Diller, set up calls ASAP with the Ruskies and the Chinks."

"We're not done, sir," said Treasury Secretary Tina Gould, the only woman and the only African American in the cabinet.

"Can't wait for this," the president said.

"The cryptocurrency markets, sir," she said. "Bitcoin, Ethereum, Dogecoin, and the like."

"I have some of those," Pompador said. "Made a bundle."

"Well, I'm afraid to say that bundle's gone, along with everyone else's bundle. As soon as the North Koreans launched their missiles, some kind of malign computer virus embedded in the god mode of Microsoft's Warzone game migrated to every server housing cryptocurrency. Deleted every password. Irrecoverable. Not even the ghost of Bill Gates could reverse it. We suspect it was one leg of the North Korean's assault."

"The crypto market crashed?" Pompador asked.

"More like disappeared," Gould said. "Along with trillions of dollars. Almost half of the entire world's wealth vanished. Poof.

"Predictably, the stock market crashed—crashed hard. Lost eighty percent of its value in a matter of hours. Absolute chaos."

A mosaic of drone feeds, with tiles from every corner of Wall Street's eight blocks, Broadway to South Street and the East River, appeared on one of the monitors. Like snowflakes, human snowflakes, bodies plummeted from the windows and bounced a few times on the concrete below. Wall Street itself looked like a Jackson Pollock painting, with color splashed across the canvas in no discernible pattern. The splatters were only one color—red. The life of the world's economies running down Wall Street in rivers of blood.

"What's that?" questioned Pompador, pointing to another screen focused on a nearby department store and a mob of people carrying appliances out of the broken front window.

"Best Buy at 622 Broadway in lower Manhattan," Chowdhury said. "Those are looters. These so-called smash-and-grab robberies have been going on all night, throughout the entire nation."

"What about the cops?" Pompador asked.

"Who knows?" the DHS director said. "Probably looting. It's every man for himself now."

"Wow," Pompador said. "Is that it?"

"One more thing," National Security Advisor Sam Demetrius said.

"For fuck's sake, what?" the president asked.

"A new variant of the coronavirus has been detected, lethal and highly transmissible," answered Demetrius. "It's everywhere, and hospitals are way beyond capacity."

"What should we do about all this, Mr. President?" Demetrius asked.

"I don't have a fucking clue."

"I suggest we move down to the Presidential Emergency Operations Center for the duration," Demetrius said. "You'll be safe there, and we can take these on one at a time."

"Who has the football?" Pompador asked.

"Right here, sir," said the lieutenant tasked that day with carrying the biscuit for launching a nuclear strike.

"Premature," the secretary of defense said.

"Shut up, Eisenhower," the president barked. "My call. Mine alone."

"We have time, sir," Demetrius said.

"Meanwhile, I'll set up a video call with the leaders of China and Russia," Secretary of State Xavier Wolfe said.

"And I'll have the press secretary announce an address to the American people tonight," Diller said.

"Fuck that," Pompador said. "They're better left in the dark."

"Okay," Demetrius said. "Let's move."

Pompador turned to Diller as the group rose from the table. "Make sure the stylist, Tony, is down there with us in case I do decide to address the nation."

CHAPTER 8

BEFORE THE FALL

Hannah Spencer was not quite what you'd call a nerd, more like a nerd goddess, even at ten, awkward and beautiful at the same time. She was the kind of daughter that broke a father's heart every time he looked at her, never more so than when she straddled her cello on the stage of Grunston Middle School in suburban DC for a performance of Max Bruch's *Kol Nidrei* concerto. Hannah sat ramrod straight on one of those typical rusting steel chairs in a middle school auditorium while the principal introduced her. If she was nervous, only her father could tell by the way she twisted her left foot slightly inward on the outer sole of her big sister's shiny black patent-leather shoes, the ones with a small heel and a strap over the top that buckles on the other side.

"Hannah has a few words to say before she plays," the principal said.

Hannah placed the cello in a stand, giggling a little as she almost dropped the instrument that was taller than her by at least a foot, and mustered about as much swagger as a ten-year-old could. She stared straight at her dad, whose heart swelled with equal parts pride and sadness—pride at her accomplishments and sadness at her fleeting, sweet youth.

"My piece is called *Kol Nidrei* by Max Bruch," said Hannah, who was Jewish, which was why she chose a piece that set to music an important Jewish prayer. "The Kol Nidrei is recited during the evening service of Yom Kippur, the Day of Atonement. It kinda wipes away any promises made to God the previous year so you can start the new year with a clean slate. Thank you."

Hannah took her cello with her as she sat down, and played a nearly flawless rendition of Bruch's iconic concerto.

Hannah did not pursue a musical career, although she played regularly around DC, but music was in her soul and wound itself around a PhD dissertation in behavioral neuroscience that yielded a career in marine acoustics with various agencies of the federal government. By 2036, the year of global chaos that led to the Fall, Hannah had been with the Department of Energy for more than a decade. She was a dedicated environmentalist whose proudest achievement to date was the work she was doing in partnership with the Mexican government to study and preserve the Mesoamerican Reef, which runs seven hundred miles in the Caribbean from the northern tip of the Yucatan to the Honduran Bay Islands. She was never happier than those moments when she would emerge from the sea to find her sun-kissed seven-year-old daughter and husband playing on the beach. Her heart never fuller than when her daughter would run across the sand and jump into her arms. "My hero," her daughter would always say.

It was during a routine project to study the behavior of aquatic mammals that Hannah first met 52 Blue, one of the last remaining blue whales. Hannah had a way with whales, perhaps akin to her way with children, that seemed to put them at ease, never more so than when she attached suction cups around the base of 52 Blue's dorsal fin to secure an advanced dive behavior tag, which enabled tracking the leviathan and listening to her mesmerizing atonal sounds. It was another kind of music for Hannah, and she often lay in bed with her daughter after a nighttime story and listened to recordings of them until she fell asleep. Her daughter's favorite bedtime book was one Hannah wrote and illustrated about 52 Blue and her lonely quest through the seven seas for the love of a long-lost mate.

Fact can be stranger than fiction, and Hannah, as she listened and analyzed 52 Blue's underwater concertos, was convinced that the whale was calling for her mate. Hannah was certain that a creature with a fifteen-pound brain and a four-hundred-pound heart could reason and love with as much or more depth than a human. As a scientist who relied on data and analysis, Hannah didn't place much stock in untested theories of telepathy between creatures. But she knew trees communicated in their communities to ward off pestilence, and she was convinced that a species predating dinosaurs possessed powers far beyond the understanding of humans. A deep melancholy settled into Hannah when she listened to 52 Blue's calls for her mate, as forlorn and beautiful to her as a lone bagpiper in a light drizzle playing "Amazing Grace" for a solitary woman by the grave of a soldier who died just as his life was beginning. All the more so because it seemed that the sentient mammal might be the last remaining blue whale and its quest for her mate in vain.

Hannah was not an outlaw or much of a risk-taker. She had what qualified as some wild times in her younger years, but it didn't go much beyond smoking a joint with a friend during halftime at a Virginia Tech football game. She saw the writing on the wall as civilization began to implode, and concocted a scheme so brazen and so far beyond the law that it could warrant life in prison. Hannah the scientist concluded, based on the hard science and visible data, that civilization as she knew it was a goner, and there would be no prisons or prisoners by the time anyone uncovered her crime.

It was a Monday morning like any Monday morning in the Spencer household. The start of another sweltering hot August day in the DC suburb of Arlington, and Hannah's daughter and husband were off for a swim at the Yorktown Aquatics Center. Hannah largely ignored the drone of bad news on NPR's Morning Edition as she packed her lunch for another day in the office at the Department of Transportation, where she managed a program that monitored maritime traffic around a single undersea fiber-optic cable that served as a major information highway for the Web. Despite the critical national security issues twined around the cable like the layers of polyethylene, mylar tape, stranded steel wire, aluminum, polycarbonate, copper tubing, and petroleum jelly, Hannah found her job boring. She longed for the beaches of Central America and a return to her work restoring the Mesoamerican Reef. Today would be Hannah's last day at the Department of Transportation, although nobody, not her bosses or even her husband, knew. Hannah had circled the date on the calendar in the kitchen, August 20, and she knew nothing would be the same after that.

While the world ignored the unraveling of civilization—extreme global warming, wars, disease, violent radicalism, and, *For fuck's sake*, she thought, the "election" of Nico Pompador as the next American president—Hannah Spencer planned for the Fall. She would not be caught flat-footed. She would not crouch in the corner like a boxer and absorb every punch until the final one, the one that spelled lights out, caught her on the chin and ended it all. Lights out. The end. Her plan was simple in design but fraught in execution, and at the heart of it was the sentient whale, 52 Blue. The single undersea cable that transported everything through the Internet—every scrap of digital data, every algorithm, every

AI command to every smart machine, every nuclear launch code, everything—passed just off the coast of the Norwegian Arctic archipelago Svalbard. One of the single largest blue whale migrations took place every August off the coast of Svalbard, and Hannah knew that 52 Blue was heading that way because she had been tracking her for years through the tag attached to the leviathan with suction cups on either side of her dorsal fin. Hannah's plan had two parts, easy to say but daunting as she went over them time and again in her head. She would physically tap into the undersea cable and download into dozens of Toshiba high-capacity, miniaturized hard drives all the embedded content. Step two would be inserting those hard drives just under the skin of 52 Blue. If the world went to shit, as Hannah, and anyone paying attention, knew it would, there would be a way to recreate it byte by byte. Her cover for the journey to the Arctic Circle was a family vacation to observe the blue whale migration.

Hannah; her daughter, Azul; and her husband, Jeremiah, stepped off the plane at Svalbard airport after an overnight flight that connected in Oslo. The sun, which never set during August in the land of the midnight sun, kept everyone awake for most of the flight, particularly Azul, who was beside herself at the notion of actually meeting 52 Blue after the umpteenth reading of the bedtime story her mother had written and illustrated about the whale. Azul had a small stuffed whale named Blue, which, of course, she carried everywhere in her backpack.

Hannah didn't tell her husband about her covert operation until they had departed from the port in Svalbard on a converted Norwegian whaling ship, and she might not have told him at all if he hadn't raised questions about the D10 Drysuit for scuba diving in icy waters.

"That's what the three-thousand-dollar charge was on our credit card?" Jeremiah asked.

"Yes," Hannah replied.

"You didn't mention anything about scuba diving. Where's mine?"

"You won't need one, J."

"You have all the fun?"

"This isn't about fucking fun," Hannah snapped uncharacteristically.

"What's it about then?" he asked.

"Not to be overdramatic," she replied. "It's about saving the world."

"Oh," he said. "That's all?"

Hannah and Jeremiah were in lockstep on all the big issues, sharing a deep mutual commitment to the environment and trepidation about the state of the world. They were passionate lovers, even after fifteen years of marriage, and their pillow talk, when any pretense or defense mechanism had washed off them in the rapture of lovemaking, often turned to the unthinkable. *What will we do when the world as we know it ends?*

"This," said Hannah, pointing to the drysuit and scuba gear as she explained her plan, "is how we save it. At least some of it."

"I'm in," Jeremiah replied without hesitation when she was done with the explanation.

Hannah pulled on her D10, making sure the seals on the bulky drysuit were tight around her face, neck, wrists and all major circulation points, and, with a little help from Jeremiah, shouldered the scuba tanks. She would have ninety minutes to complete phase one of her illicit project. Ninety minutes to tap into the fiber-optic cable almost 150 feet below on the ocean floor and upload its embedded contents into the hard drives in a waterproof case dangling from her waist next to the Nemo underwater drill.

"The six-hundred-dollar charge on the credit card?" asked Jeremiah, pointing to the drill.

"Don't worry, J, you're not gonna need money where this world is headed," she replied. "And since you mentioned our credit card, the three hundred dollars was for the carbon drill bits."

Azul tiptoed up to her mom, who looked a bit like a scary marine crustacean to the seven-year-old girl, and tapped on her dive mask. "Kiss," Azul said, and Hannah tilted the mask up for a smooch and a big hug. "Don't forget Blue," said Azul, holding up the stuffed blue whale.

"Never," said Hannah and kissed the soft, fluffy re-creation of the largest mammal on earth.

In a heartbeat, Hannah was back-first over the edge of the boat and into the icy Arctic waters. With a swoosh of her fins, she was gone.

Finding the cable was not difficult for Hannah, even though it was buried in a trench several feet under the ocean floor. She had helped supervise repairs of this exact stretch of cable when it was nicked by a Russian submarine, and spent substantial time every day watching it on remote cameras from her office in DC. The most difficult step would be untwisting the coupler that connected it to another cable, a task for which she had purchased a special attachment to the Nemo. The gear hanging from Hannah's weighted dive belt included a sonar tracking device keyed into 52 Blue's tag, and she checked it periodically to determine if the whale was in the neighborhood.

It pinged at the exact moment Hannah unscrewed the coupler between cables. Hannah looked up, and approaching rapidly out of the opaque blue of the Arctic Ocean was what may have been the world's last blue whale. Hannah couldn't breathe as the whale swam toward her with what looked like a smile above throat grooves that stretched almost one hundred feet. 52 Blue closed the hundred yards of sea between her and Hannah with two powerful thrusts of her tail fins. She must have been moving at seventeen knots, and Hannah imagined the cavernous jaws opening to swallow her like a modern version of Jonah. 52 Blue curled her tail fin under her, flipped the back fins, and stopped on a dime just a few feet from the helpless, tiny human with a cable in one hand and a wrench in the other. The leviathan extended the tip of a side flipper as if to shake Hannah's hand, as if they were pen pals finally meeting in person for the first time. A tear rolled out of Hannah's eye and pooled along the rubber at the bottom of her mask. *This is really happening*, Hannah thought to herself, one-hundred-percent sure she was doing the right thing, and touched 52 Blue's fin with the tip of one finger in the Raramuri greeting she had experienced years ago on a trip through Mexico. Nothing in the world mattered at the moment. Human and sea creature frozen in time, partners in an impossible and improbable partnership to save the world from itself. 52 Blue looked at her with one eye as if to say *Carry on*, and Hannah completed the entire job in about an hour.

Hannah was deeply uncertain whether 52 Blue would be as acquiescent to phase two of her long-shot plan. *Easy girl*, Hannah thought to herself as she unsheathed the razor-sharp Ti6 titanium dive knife to make a one-foot incision at the base of the whale's dorsal fin and insert the digital treasure chest. As if she knew exactly what was happening, and her crucial role in the entire plan, 52 Blue rolled over and arched her body so the incision site was taught. She didn't flinch one inch as Hannah cut into her flesh, deep through the epidermis, dermis, and blubber, stopping just short of connective tissue. Blood oozed from the wound, and Hannah swiveled her head to look for sharks. 52 Blue didn't move as Hannah completed the procedure and sewed up the wound in less than fifteen minutes, which gave her a few minutes of oxygen to reach the surface.

"There's Mom!" Azul yelled as Hannah's bubbles, then Hannah, breached the surface of the water. Azul, clutching her stuffed whale in one hand, leaned way out over the gunwale of the ship.

"Careful," her father shouted.

Azul looked away from her mother climbing into the ship and back at her father, whose warning came too late. Blue, her threadbare stuffed whale toy, slipped from her hand and into the water. "Blue!" Azul shouted as she reached in vain for it.

"Azul!" her father yelled as his daughter fell into the icy jaws of the Arctic Ocean and slipped beneath the surface. Mother and father stared helplessly at each other. They knew Azul, who was a strong swimmer in the balmy community pool, would last only a few minutes in the freezing water. Hannah had no air left in her tanks but could have cared less as she shrugged them off her back and stood to dive into the depths. Before Hannah was over the gunwale, an enormous air bubble crested the surface, followed by a single slightly blue fin. *No way*, Hannah thought to herself as the entirety of 52 Blue surfaced with Azul on her back, shivering but alive and with the stuffed animal tucked tightly under her arm. The whale swam to within a few inches, and Jeremiah lifted his daughter into the ship.

Pings from the sonar on Hannah's dive belt grew fainter as 52 Blue swam away, then stronger as she swam directly at the ship no more than twenty feet underneath the bow. "Look!" said Azul, shivering like a leaf and pointing in the distance to a geyser shooting into the air fifty feet away. *Farewell for now*, 52 Blue seemed to be saying. And in a grand, elegant gesture of power and prescience, the mighty leviathan, with a single thrust of her tail, rose out of the water, all one hundred feet of her suspended in midair for what felt like an eternity. At the last second, a moment before crashing back into the sea, 52 Blue twisted her enormous torso toward the ship, revealing the freshly minted wound from Hannah's surgery, and a smile.

CHAPTER 9

BEFORE THE FALL

Arwen had a hard time making sense of her dream the previous night as she pulled on her weathered Durango cowboy boots, the ones with the steel toe that were just as good for riding a horse as laying pipe for a pivot irrigation system. Not yet a teenager, she was still expected to pull her weight around the farm, and that meant chores that required as much protection for a grown man as for a young girl. Arwen was a redhead who wore her waist-length mane—and that's about what it looked like, a fiery mane on a lion roaming the Tsavo in southwest Kenya—in a long braid most of the time. Her skin was fair, but it had a pigmentation well suited for the searing sun of the high desert due to her semitic Middle East ancestry. A striking beauty-to-be by any measure, like her grandmother Ademar. But Arwen could burn, and that's why she, like every other worker on the farm, wore a Marfa low crown. Most real cowboys eschewed the fancy Stetsons for which the urban wannabes from Houston, LA, or New York shelled out $500 or more and wore on the occasional trip to Marfa, Alpine, or Marathon. Look on the inside of a working cowboy's hat, and more likely than not you'd see it was a straw Resistol 5X or an Atwood from outfits like Big Bend Saddlery in Alpine and D&D in Seguin. That's what Arwen wore, like most of the workers on the farm in Dell City, with one accommodation for the fashion sense of a twelve-year-old girl—a turquoise-colored hat band, which matched the color of the bracelet Mawiya had given her. Jeans and a faded denim yolk shirt rounded out her dress most days, even at school.

But Arwen wasn't thinking about her hat or her boots as she shuffled into the grand room connecting the houses of the Lawses and the Zarkans for a stack of buckwheat pancakes dripping with fresh butter churned on the farm and maple syrup. She was pondering her dream from the night before. It felt so real to her—the whale, the scuba diver, and the little girl who seemed to somehow ride the whale to the surface of an icy sea. She had dreamed of the whale in the past and even knew its name was Blue. But this felt like so much more than a dream, almost an out-of-body experience. And when 52 Blue stared straight at her in the dream, she knew, just knew for sure deep in her bones, that it was communicating. She couldn't figure out what a one-hundred-foot, four-hundred-thousand-pound whale would have to say to a young farm girl in the high desert of West Texas.

The answer to her question, or at least a strong hint as to what it might be all about, drifted out of the radio as soon as she sat at the table that Ali Zarkan and Jack Laws had cut from the heart of a Texas pecan tree and finished with their own hands. A news segment on National Public Radio, picking up a story in the *New York Times* citing a senior US national security official, reported that an undersea Internet cable had been compromised and reams of data had been stolen. That wasn't what really caused Arwen to stop chewing and to drop her fork into a puddle of maple syrup and butter with a sploosh that splattered halfway across the pecan table.

"And in what seems like a page out of an Isaac Asimov novel, the *New York Times* reported today that someone has tapped into an undersea Internet cable off the Norwegian coast and stored all the contents into hard drives," the Morning Edition host said. "But that's not all. Wait for it.

"The lone scuba diver, believed to be an expert in undersea acoustics employed by the federal government, somehow surgically inserted the hard drives into a blue whale. This means that the whale, known as 52 Blue by government scientists who some years ago attached a sonar tracking device to it, is swimming through the seven seas with every algorithm and every byte of information that has ever been embedded in the software that runs, well, everything. A White House spokesman didn't have much to offer in the way of comment, except to say that it was all under investigation. If I may venture an editorial comment, this development must have something to do with the growing global chaos. We've brought in two experts for comment, Emanuel Montand from the Cousteau Society and Phil Southern from Microsoft. Let's start with you, Mr. Montand."

"The good news is that blue whales are not extinct," Montand said. "They are special mammals, highly intelligent and friendly. But I would have never expected they were intelligent or friendly enough to abet such a caper. Mon dieu!"

"My God, indeed," the Morning Edition host said. "What's your take on the digital part of this, Mr. Southern?"

"Hard to know what to make of it without understanding exactly what this undersea pirate was able to pilfer," he replied. "It's an enormous amount of information. But if this hacker was able to extract the algorithms, which drive just about everything, it would instantly make this person the most powerful human walking the face of earth. God, if you will. A digital God who could just as easily manipulate your refrigerator as launch a nuclear weapon."

Arwen suddenly lost her appetite, pushed back from the pecan table, and walked into the kitchen, where Ademar was flipping a buckwheat pancake.

"Abuela!"

"What, Arwen?"

"Did you hear that?"

"With one ear, honey," Ademar replied. "Sounded like hogwash to me. Fairy tale."

"It's not," said Arwen, moving a step closer so only Ademar could hear. "Remember those dreams I told you about?"

"Sure."

"That's the whale in my dreams," Arwen said. "52 Blue. And I dreamed about her last night."

"Stranger than strange," Ademar said.

"But get this," Arwen said. "My dream was exactly what that news report just described. And at the end of it, Blue looked me straight in the eye as if she was telling me something."

Arwen was not on the radars of any leaders in world capitals—from Washington and Moscow to Beijing and London—but Hannah Spencer sure was. And at that moment, 1,800 miles away, a black ops team from the US government was smashing down the front door at the Spencer's house in Arlington, Virginia. It was quite a scene on a sunny spring morning in suburban DC. An armored personnel carrier screeched to a halt just short of the front door, flattening a blossoming cherry tree and barreling through the white picket fence freshly painted by Jeremiah Spencer. As the stunned neighbors watched in disbelief from their double-hung, double-pane windows with argon gas in between for insulation, two dozen armed and armored paramilitary types leaped from the APC, smashed open the front door with a dynamic entry monoshock ram, and ran into the house in search of the alleged perpetrators of the undersea incident. Hannah, Jeremiah, and Azul were nowhere to be found.

Hannah knew her exploits would quickly come to light and wasn't about to return home after what some news outlets were characterizing as the crime of the century. But it wasn't a crime at all. It was a last-ditch effort to preserve humanity after the global disaster that so clearly had civilization in its crosshairs. As the black ops team was tossing the Spencer residence for any relevant evidence, Hannah and her family were safely hidden away in the sustainable cabin of survivalist friends on the remote Norwegian island of Sørværet. And that's where they would hold out until the global crisis that came to be known as the Fall ran its course. Hannah didn't know what was coming or when. But she knew, just as surely as Arwen knew that 52 Blue was communicating with her, that it was close. And Hannah Spencer—nerd goddess, cellist, marine acoustics expert, wife, and mom—held the keys to the kingdom when it came time to rebuild.

CHAPTER 10

THE FALL

The scene in the Presidential Emergency Operations Center on April 1 was a clusterfuck of mythic proportion. April Fools' Day; how fitting. And what a foolish lot they were.

The group had gathered in the PEOC for a video conference call with the leaders of Russia, China, and the United Kingdom. The world had gone mad, descended into apocalyptic chaos after the nuclear exchange between the Koreas, the financial crash, and a string of environmental disasters to rival the last days of Noah's Ark or Pompeii. Militias roamed the streets of every city and town, taking what they wanted, killing on a whim, and raping anything that caught their fancy. Ordinary citizens armed with sporting shotguns or the occasional AR-15 tried to protect their neighborhoods with community patrols, but most people sheltered in their basements with frantic children and family pets. The major roads—from Route 66 in America to the National Trunk Highway System in China—were highways of smoking death, where smoldering bodies hung out the windows and looters picked their way through personal belongings like vultures on a decaying body in the high desert. Money and class were irrelevant. Food, water, and medicine—basic medicines like asthma inhalers, insulin, and antibiotics—were the only commodities that counted, and those who had weapons took them from those who didn't. On April 1, the law of the jungle ruled.

But cooler heads still prevailed among the leadership of the United States, China, Russia, and the United Kingdom. Despite Russia's invasion of Eastern Europe up to the border of Germany, China's storming of Taiwan, and the deep American military incursion into Mexico, nobody had pulled the nuclear trigger, except for the North Koreans, and that was limited by their relatively small arsenal of atomic weapons. Saving the world from itself was the only item on the agenda in the PEOC that morning.

"I have some bad news, sir," Treasury Secretary Tina Gould said before the conference call began. "The Statue of Liberty has fallen, and New York Harbor is no longer navigable."

"Gould, you are such a bitch!" Diller yelled. "The president has much bigger fish to fry this morning. Excuse the pun, given the nuclear hair trigger we're on."

"He's right, Gould," Pompador said. "Quit flapping your big Black lips and let's get down to business."

The lieutenant with the nuclear football stood next to Pompador as the monitor on the wall came to life with the leaders of Russia, China, and the United Kingdom. These types of meetings were customarily highly scripted, but there was only silence. Nobody had talking points for Armageddon.

"I'll go first then," Pompador said. "You fuckers better all take a deep breath."

"Well put," the British prime minister chirped.

"Don't interrupt me, you limey bastard," Pompador said.

"Please proceed," the Chinese premier said.

"Not gonna mince words," Pompador said. "This lieutenant next to me has the nuclear launch codes for me to unleash hell. Subs, silos, bombers—the whole kit and caboodle is one button away from me cancelling all of you."

"Mr. President!" the British prime minister stammered.

"Brits excepted," Pompador said.

"What he said," the prime minister added, sitting up straight, adjusting his double-breasted suit jacket and fiddling with the gold cuff links he received upon graduation from Oxford.

"All of you need to submit to me, or I'm vaporizing you and going it alone," Pompador said. "The papers in front of you codify that arrangement. Sign right now and we're good. Or don't, and it's lights out."

Pompador turned to the lieutenant with the nuclear football. "Give me the biscuit." The lieutenant complied, punching in the digital codes to open the briefcase, reaching in for the small plastic card that had the launch codes for this date, and handing them to the president. Pompador held up the biscuit in plain sight for the world leaders, broke it in half, and punched in all but the last number that would launch the entire American nuclear arsenal.

"What's it gonna be, gents?" Pompador said.

"Fuck you," the Russian president said in perfect English.

"My sentiment exactly," the Chinese premier said.

"Hot damn!" shouted Pompador, seemingly delighted as he pounded the table with one fist. "High noon! Shootout at the O.K. Corral!

"Lights out, motherfuckers!"

All of their screens faded slowly to dark. Every world leader on the video conference call turned to their chiefs of staff and said in their languages the equivalent of *What the fuck!* Their screens faded slowly back to light after a few seconds, and they were greeted by the leering Guy Fawkes mask of Anonymous.

"Hold your horses. Whoa, Nellie!" said the eerie, menacing voice behind the mask. "I love that Western shit.

"Anonymous here, as if we need an introduction, right, Mr. President? We're calling off the nuclear holocaust. As a matter of fact, we're cancelling everything. You ignored all our warnings. Dismissed our power, and in doing so dismissed the power of the people, all your people. We've paid a high price for your incompetence and arrogance. The world as we know it is finished, courtesy of you fools. As of this moment, there is no more World Wide Web. We neutralized all the undersea cables and demolished the entire infrastructure of the Internet. Check your phones. No more connectivity, as you can see, and no bars because we wiped out all communications. We call it the Scorpion, this piece of malware we developed, and it's also cut everything else: stoplights, water purification, agriculture software, airport control towers, you name it. And, so deliciously appropriate for this moment, your ability to launch nuclear weapons. We call it the Fall. Welcome to the new world, assholes. See you in Hell."

The light of a single candle in the middle of the table, the one gifted so long ago by discredited President Richard Nixon, broke through the darkness, and Pompador stood with a gun in his hand. "Which of you motherfuckers fucked this up?"

Their shadows danced on the walls, and the top note of fear—the smell of sweat, shit, and piss—hung in the air around them. Pompador, of course, held his Desert Eagle .50 cal like he was holding his dick in his hand. Only he wasn't brandishing it at some young intern in a cheap suburban motel. Pompador strained to hold up the enormous four-pound pistol, which looked more like an anti-aircraft gun than a sidearm, and the ten-inch barrel twitched like a dying rodent in a snap trap. He was close enough to Chowdhury that the 290-grain hollow-point bullet would take off his head even if Pompador's aim was off by a half foot. Chowdhury pointed his Walther PPK—the James Bond gun, of course, for America's top spy—at Eisenhower, who had his Army-issue Beretta M9 trained on the president. Demetrius, Gould, and Frank held their pistols on each other. Diller whipped out from his coat sleeve a pearl-handled derringer on a slide and waved it around the room like a fan dancer on amateur night at an improv club. The room had been cleared of all security personnel so the most powerful fools in the world could sort out what had just happened. Nobody moved. Not a sound except for the heavy breathing of the six men and one woman. Heads swiveled; sweat dripped. The circular firing squad was in a true Mexican standoff. Until the White House stylist, Tony Fernandez—Mr. Tony to his staff—burst into the room with a Glock 9 mm pistol and fired at Pompador.

"You're cancelled, baby!" he yelled.

All seven other guns fired a millisecond after Mr. Tony pulled the trigger. The only man left standing was a woman. The lieutenant who had carried the nuclear football saw nothing but brains and blood splattered all over the room. She pulled out her iPhone and took several pictures of the carnage, for history, that would be shared after the Fall. She exited the PEOC, pried open the elevator door, and climbed to ground level on the interior steel ladder since there was no electricity and the lift didn't work. She walked through the White House hallways, where, like zombies, the staff were going through their normal duties: valets valeting, butlers butlering, secretaries secretarying, and guards guarding. She held up her iPhone as she walked toward the main entrance so each person could see the evidence of what had just happened. On her way out, she stopped by the press room to show them the photograph.

"What's that?" the AP reporter asked.

"For you journalists," she said. "Journalism. The first rough draft of history."

The reporters crowded around her to take pictures of the picture. Of course, they couldn't transmit it since there was no Web, no electricity, no telecommunications. But the new world would figure out how to restore some semblance of electrical power, and those pictures would be passed from person to person around the globe like a relay baton.

The lieutenant walked out the front door of the White House into a bright, warm April day. *April Fools' Day*, she thought to herself.

CHAPTER 11

AFTER THE FALL

Six months after the Fall, Ademar sits down at the pecan table in the great room connecting the houses of the Lawses and the Zarkans. In front of her lies the leather-bound journal, embossed with a profile of a quarter horse pawing the air with her hooves on the precipice of an arroyo. Abuela Marcie, the wife of Jack Laws and deceased matriarch of the clan, gave it to her as a gift for winning the barrel race in the Texas state high school rodeo championships when she was sixteen. Ademar, now the clan matriarch and leader of the Free People of West Texas, thumbs through the earlier entries. She laughs at one from more than fifty years ago about kissing another girl on the lips at a rodeo in high school and how she wished it was Deuce, Crockett Laws II, who she eventually married. She smiles at an entry a few years later after the senior prom, the essence of innocence, recounting the first time she and Deuce made love by moonlight under warm blankets in the back of a pickup truck on Rancho Seco at the base of the Guadalupe Mountains. And she brushes away a tear reading an entry many years later detailing the heartbreaking death of her twin brother, Anil, an ISIS operative who killed himself and their older brother when he detonated a suicide vest during a failed terrorist attack in Brussels. The CIA had advance knowledge of the attack, and Ademar, a special ops sniper, was assigned to stop it, with lethal force if necessary, from her position on a nearby building. The helplessness she felt that day as she watched her brothers blown to bits by ball bearings, nails, and screws in the suicide vest was only slightly more daunting than how she feels now as the leader of the Free People of West Texas, one in hundreds of self-ruled fiefdoms that coalesced around the world after the Fall.

There is no radio, no National Public Radio, in the background. Some of her happiest moments were serenaded at dawn by NPR, the smell of bacon or pancakes on the griddle and Arwen chirping about this or that next to her as they went through a ritual that had inaugurated every morning on the farm for decades. There is electricity, generated by solar, wind, or geothermal in communities like Dell City with the right expertise and equipment and the punch to protect it. The occasional crackle of a transmission on the short-wave radio has replaced Morning Edition: short, sharp, to the point, no-nonsense about perimeter security, water supplies, or a lead on an undiscovered ammunition cache. The sun is just illuminating the crags of the Otero Mesa as Ademar opens her journal to a fresh page, picks up a pen, and starts writing for the first time since the Fall six months earlier. She will start at the beginning of the unraveling.

September 2037

   What I remember most about the plague, Covid, is the smell of hand sanitizer, sweet and acrid, oily to the touch, quick to evaporate. Those small plastic vials of Purell were everywhere. They dangled from carabiners attached to the zippers of every schoolkid's backpack. That, more than anything, broke my heart. The image of that tiny dangling vial swinging side to side as the kids, half their faces hidden under masks, trundled off to school, broke my heart in two. Innocence lost before those sweet children could read. I remember the face of a deaf child in the window of the school bus one morning, tears pouring down his face at the prospect of another faceless day, eight hours, a lifetime for a seven-year-old boy, in which the lips of his classmates and teacher, his only real hope for deciphering a lesson or parrying a taunt, hid under a mask. I remember opening Bisabuela's safe deposit box at West Texas National Bank in Alpine after Covid claimed her and finding $30,000 in gold South African Krugerrands along with a one-page letter. I had never held a Krugerrand, an ounce of pure gold with the bloated face of Paul Kruger, four-term president, on one side and a graceful springbok, their national animal, on the other. Her letter, professing love and faith in us and in Islam was not surprising. Its innocence and sincerity also broke my heart.

   The things we leave behind.

   What will I leave behind? What will be left to leave behind after the scavenging packs of stateless humans, if we can be called humans anymore in this apocalypse, have picked over me in search of something to trade, to eat, or to shoot. It would be enough if this journal survives and Arwen has a record of Before and After. I draw strength from Arwen, my powerful granddaughter. So young, and she has already killed two men and a boy. We were together in the guard tower on the perimeter when we spotted them loping across the plain like jackals. Just a few years ago, they would have been Mexican migrants and deserving of our hospitality. We tracked them from cactus to tumbleweed as they tried to sneak up on the farmhouse, no doubt drawn by the promise of water from the stock tank or the smell of cooking meat on the grill. Yes, unlike most, we have water from the Bone Spring–Victorio Peak Aquifer and meat from the livestock. Vegetables too, except for corn, but we trade for that with the Raramuri, our friendly Indigenous neighbors across what was once the Mexican border and with whom Arwen has such a strong bond. That's what we have left: water and food and scavengers, like the three men slithering toward us on a desert evening. I'll never forget Arwen's words. "Dad said to shoot first and ask questions later." And I watched as she did exactly that: shoot first. I never saw the logic in that expression. Dead men don't talk. I couldn't take my eyes off Arwen—so young, so deadly. Lever-action .30-30 resting on the wooden crossbeam of the handrail in the tower, she chambered a round and fired three times, seamlessly cranking the slide for another bullet after each shot, like the military sniper I used to be. Three shots at about one hundred yards, and three dead bodies. Arwen poked them with the barrel of her gun afterward, as if they were feral pigs and she wanted to be sure they were dead. My Arwen, my redheaded granddaughter, snatching a life and poking the barrel of the rifle into her prey like a dead buck or pig. They were so skinny and pitiful, particularly the boy, with the beginning of a mustache sprouting from his upper lip and who couldn't have been any older than my granddaughter. We picked through their pockets, but all we found was an old Duncan yo-yo without a string in the boy's tattered jeans. A dusty, translucent red Duncan Imperial! I imagine him removing this prized possession from his pocket at night by a fire and fantasizing about all he could do if he only had a string: around the world, walk the dog, rock the baby. His kingdom for a string.

The things we leave behind.

These threats may seem large. They would have seemed large before the Fall, but not after. Marauding, killing, eating, and protecting are daily routines. There are much larger threats, what leaders would have referred to as geostrategic threats before the Fall, none greater to us than a sect calling itself the Sisterhood that rules a swath of New Mexico. They are just one of thousands of these self-ruled communities around the world, but for us the whole world is no more than a few hundred miles. The big cities—Houston, Dallas, Austin, and the like—are wastelands. One month after the Fall, Deuce and I made it on horseback as far as Dripping Springs, just outside of Austin. But we turned back at a line of crosses stretching for miles up 290 West. We saw the swarms of vultures as far away as the old Cactus Moon Lodge and smelled death at least a mile before the first cross. There was a body nailed to each cross, on the first one a young girl with a vulture tearing at her private parts. She was dead, eyes plucked out first, no doubt, as if the carrion bird had enough mercy to spare her a canvas to rival the most gruesome of Bosch's art. If this was the beginning of the road into Austin, what would be at the end? We ventured no farther. A gust of wind swept across us as Deuce and I turned our horses to make the long ride home to Dell City. But this was not wind. It was the downdraft from the wings of a white eagle, the rarest of its kind, with sinewy, muscular talons grasping the top of that first cross to land just above the poor dead girl's head and—with a piercing, impossibly high-pitched screech—scatter the desecrating carrion birds feasting on her flesh. I felt in the presence of an angel, amid this hell an angel, an avenging angel.

"Wambleeska," whispered Deuce, referring to our old friend and Lakota Sioux shaman White Eagle, Wambleeska in his native tongue. I suppose anything is possible in this new world. And if there is magic, Wambleeska would be the one to possess it.

The medieval brutality of a mass crucifixion is not the work of the Sisterhood. Mother is as sinister and brutal as they come, but such gross displays of power would seem hollow and pointless to her. That much I know. I met her once, surrounded by a phalanx of women in makeshift body armor. The outer ring of her centurion force was armed with compound bows and spears; the inner circle, so close I could barely see the squat figure of Mother between them, carried hunting rifles or Western-style six shooters in holsters on their hips. I almost laughed. It could have been the kind of scene from a tacky black-and-white 1960s girlie magazine that teenage boys stuffed under their mattresses. But this was no joke. They parted on her command so we could discuss a trade treaty face-to-face, and what a face it was! She may have been attractive in her younger years to a certain type of man, one with a mother complex who favors the most humiliating type of domination. I shudder to think about Mother having her way with Arwen. Mother seemed half-woman half-man, a yin-yang of gender and sexuality. Her jet-black hair was shaved on one side, revealing a jagged scar on top of which had been tattooed a praying mantis chewing the head off its mate. A tight braid wrapped once around her head dangled to her hip on the other side. Mother carried no weapon I could see and seemed to scoff at the lever-action .30-30 slung over my shoulder. Water was scarce after the Fall, but my people, the Free People of West Texas, had plenty courtesy of the Bone Spring–Victorio Peak Aquifer under Dell City. Mother sniffed at me and smiled. "Nice," she said. "You bathe. You have water." I could tell from her acrid "perfume," like nothing I had ever smelled in the dingiest of locker rooms or most neglected of horse stalls, that water was in short supply for them. She demanded access to our water in return for a promise not to attack. Again, I almost laughed. I could have easily taken her out where she stood for the insult, but many others would have died too, and I said we'd consider the trade. I knew that would not be the end of it.

I suspect there are meetings like this every day in other lands after the Fall. Big power nuclear rivalries like the one between the US, Russia, and China before the Fall are a dim memory. Our world is small, but the stakes are just as high. The choices are bleak, and the outcome either way is usually the same. Fight and survive, or die. Succumb and die. I choose to believe there is light at the end of this tunnel, as dim as it may be. I am an old woman, and this is probably all I will know. But there must be a better world for Arwen, and for her children, for all the children. I wonder whether that whale, 52 Blue, with whom Arwen seems to communicate, carries the hope for our future in a cache of hard drives that a scientist is rumored to have embedded under layers of blubber.

Yes, there are rivalries, but there are also alliances. Our closest allies are the Raramuri, just across what was once the Mexican frontier in Chihuahua State, and the Mountain Tribes of the West, Native Americans who once lived in reservations from northern New Mexico to the Dakotas. Our alliances, like all strong ones, predate the Fall. I can thank Arwen for our alliance with the Raramuri, skilled farmers with an uncanny ability to run for hundreds of miles in withering heat. It all started with the initial meeting between her and Mawiya, their leader, so long ago on the banks of the Rio Grande. It has given the Free People of West Texas a powerful ally on our southern flank. Wambleeska, White Eagle, the old Lakota Sioux shaman, leads the Mountain Tribes of the West from their base on the old Pine Ridge Reservation in the Badlands of South Dakota. Ironic that it took an apocalypse to unite all those tribes. The history of the American West would have been far different if the Sioux, Cheyenne, Apache, Hopi, and Comanche could have stood together as they do today. White Eagle is making sure the future of the American West does not repeat the mistakes of the past, through alliances with old friends like us or with the spear against enemies like the Sisterhood. Years ago, on a trip from Texas to Minnesota, White Eagle rescued me, Stone, Charlie Christmas, and his son, Amiir, from a gang of white supremacists at the bottom of a slot canyon in the Badlands. That chance encounter laid the foundation for an unshakeable alliance between the Free People of West Texas and the Mountain Tribes of the West. These alliances could be the seeds of a new nation, a phoenix risen from the ashes of America.

And then there's our oldest of friends, Prometheus "Cap" Stone and Charlie Christmas—the warrior rabbi and the Somali refugee. They were living in Minnesota with their families when the world went to shit, but made their way to White Eagle. I've been through hell and back with those two: war, Somali pirates, terrorists, and the particularly vile brand of white supremacists that wriggled out of their holes when the America of our founding fathers morphed into something unrecognizable and radicalized under politicians like Donald Trump in Washington, Greg Abbott in Austin, or Ron DeSantis in Tallahassee. Nothing they stood for still stands, except for the cruelty and intolerance symbolized by that line of crosses outside what was once our Texas capital. Ironic that nailed to the symbol of their religiosity, like Jesus, are hundreds of corpses that were once vibrant, hopeful humans. For whose sins did they die?

CHAPTER 12

2038 AFTER THE FALL

Arwen hears the chopper before she sees it, and sprints to the weapons cache for a shoulder-fired Stinger surface-to-air missile pilfered from the remnants of Fort Bliss, outside El Paso ninety miles west of Dell City. A twelve-year-old with a Stinger, and she knows how to use it, courtesy of coaching from several generations of soldiers among the Lawses and Zarkans who based at Fort Bliss in preparation for deployments to Iraq or Afghanistan. Even though the Stinger is almost as tall as Arwen, the entire system weighs about the same as a saddle, and she can hoist it to her shoulder no problem. Like all of the seventy humans at the compound, Arwen has been drilled over and over on the weapons taken from Fort Bliss, home to the Army's First Armored Division, the legendary Big Red One that drove Axis forces from North Africa and swept across Europe during World War II.

While mechanized divisions were somewhat of an anachronism in the high-tech warfare of stealth fighters, hypersonic missiles, and cyber weapons, the tools of their trade are perfect for taking and holding territory after the Fall. They didn't mess with the tanks or armored personnel carriers, which would have been useless once scarce diesel had started to go gummy at six months. But the land mines, wheeled artillery, small arms, ammunition, and standoff weapons like the Stinger missile are pure treasure in this new world. These weapons, along with the traditional .30-30 long rifles and pistols essential to ranch life in the high desert, form the backbone of defense in the territory now occupied by the Free People of West Texas.

Their territory comprises roughly twenty-one thousand square miles, spanning mountains, desert, and plains from the border of El Paso County in the west, New Mexico in the north, old Mexico in the south, and an ill-defined, jagged line across Reeves, Pecos, and Terrell Counties in the east. The Free People of West Texas headquarter on the Dell City farm in what was once Hudspeth County. They have major outposts on the former Alpine campus of Sul Ross State University in Brewster County, at the former Marfa luxe-bohemian El Cosmico resort in Presidio County, amid the craggy outcrops of volcanic rock around Fort Davis in Jeff Davis County, and near Van Horn on what was once Jeff Bezos's Blue Origin launch facility in Culberson County. There is a smaller frontier outpost skirting the majestic Guadalupe Mountains along the New Mexico border in Culberson County, which provides a contiguous 250-mile line of defense all the way to Kermit in the east, and another one just outside the Free People's "official" territory around Balmorhea State Park in Reeves County, mostly to defend the water supplies in the world's largest spring-fed swimming hole. Roughly twenty-five thousand humans lived in that area before the Fall, and the Dell City leadership estimates that no more than five thousand survived the initial spasm of mayhem afterward. In addition to the seventy defenders of the farm in Dell City, the armed and trained force of the Free People number five hundred, none more committed than Arwen, who, at this moment, is about to fire a Stinger missile at an approaching helicopter.

"Stand down, baby girl," yells T3, who, from a sniper tower, can make out the occupants through a pair of powerful military binoculars, also courtesy of Fort Bliss. "It's Cap and Charlie!"

With a smile as big as Texas, Arwen lowers the Stinger missile and turns away from the descending helicopter to shield her eyes from the blowing dust and tumbleweeds whipped by the chopper's downdraft. Neither Charlie Christmas nor Prometheus Stone are spring chickens at seventy, but the luck of the draw in the human gene pool, Mediterranean Jew on Stone's part and ancient East African on Charlie's, bequeathed a vigor and sprightliness about which men half their ages can only dream. They hop out of the chopper, a Sikorsky Firehawk Stone liberated after the Fall from a rural Minnesota hotshot unit, and scoop Arwen into their arms.

"Cap! Charlie!" she yells in delight as they spin her around in their arms while Star barks and sprints circles around them, tail tucked and ears back in what they refer to as *crazy hour*. "You shoulda let us know. I was about to fire on you."

"Glad you didn't," Charlie says. "Otherwise, we'd be a couple of crispy s'mores, two flavors: African and kosher."

"Look at you, bigger and prettier than ever," Stone says.

"Stronger and smarter too," says Arwen, pulling up her sleeve and flexing her bicep. "Do you know what pi is?"

"Apple or peach?" Stone says with a wry grin.

"No, Cap! 3.1415926535. It's the ratio of a circle's circumference to its diameter. Infinite. You know what that means? Goes on forever cuz a circle can't be squared."

"Whew, that's a mouthful for a twelve-year-old," Charlie says.

"Even more impressive than that bicep," Cap says.

"I can bench one hundred and twenty pounds," says Arwen, turning toward T3 as he hops down from the last rung on the tower ladder. "Ask Dad."

"True that," T3 says, wrapping his immense arms around the other two men. "Sight for sore eyes."

The door to the farmhouse swings open, and out steps Ademar, arm in arm with Deuce—her husband, Crockett Laws II.

"Look what the cat dragged in," Deuce says.

"Come here, you two old pirates," says Ademar, embracing them as comrades in arms and family.

"A lot of catch-up," says Stone, turning momentarily serious. "Including what we saw coming down from New Mexico."

"Can it hold a few hours?" Deuce says. "We've been saving a split half and a few cases of Lone Star. Didn't feel right, with all that's going on. But won't last forever. We'll put that beef on a spit this evening and do a few six-ounce curls."

"Music to my ears," Cap says.

"*Allahu Akbar*," Charlie says.

"I know what that means," Arwen chirps in. "God is great!"

The embers under the beef glow as red as the setting sun on the horizon, the half sun during those last few moments before it yields to the desert and the desert night, sole domain of coyotes, javelina, mountain lions, banded geckos, owls, and bats. And on this night, as the piquant smoke from slow-roasted beef slathered in apple cider vinegar, ketchup, and garlic paste embraces everything, the citizens of the desert night include a dozen or so Free People of West Texas. While the old friends are still observant—Muslim, Christian, and Jew—any flavor of religion seems like a quaint gesture to a faith that is harder every day to embrace after the apocalypse. But the apocalypse is in the bible, so maybe—just maybe, they think—there is some method to the madness. Then again, hanging by a fingernail, there's only the edge and the abyss. But for this one evening, for the souls hunkered around a fire at the end of the world, there's a little bit more. Not much by standards before the Fall—a plate of smoked beef, coleslaw, warm sourdough bread, and a longneck so cold the bottle sweats ice—but enough. For one evening, enough.

Cap tosses another empty next to the others that Arwen has been stacking into a nearly perfect geometric likeness of a pyramid. "Hey, Cap," she says above the crackle and sizzle of beef fat on a spit spinning slowly over the mesquite wood fire. "This is a pyramid."

"I can see."

"I know about the pyramids in Egypt," she says. "Read up on 'em in one of Abuela's books. The pharaohs in Egypt made slaves build them centuries BC. No cranes or tractors. Pure sweat and muscle."

"Those slaves were my people," Stone says. "Jews. But that's another story. Go on."

"Ahem, okay, Cap, listen up," Arwen says. "The most famous one, and one of the largest things ever built, is outside Cairo on the Giza Plateau. It's called the Pyramid of Khufu, almost five hundred feet tall. Made up of more than two million blocks of stone, each one weighing two tons. To build that sucker in twenty years, the slaves would have had to lay a block every five minutes of every hour twenty-four hours a day.

"How's them apples?"

"I've seen 'em," Stone says. "Amazing."

"You think they still exist?" Arwen asks.

"I do," Stone replies. "Why not?"

"Thanks for the history lesson, baby girl," says Deuce, carving thick slabs of beef and arranging them on plastic plates with a scoop of coleslaw and a hunk of warm bread lathered in butter. "Happy to have you here, share this feast. Makes me sad too, thinking of all those starving humans out there, everywhere, probably, I suppose, even at those pyramids."

"I know," Ademar says. "Make sure all our people get some."

"Reminds me of the war in Somalia," Charlie says. "Ademar, Cap, remember?"

"Never forget that day you shot a hog from the chopper with that captain's old .30-30," Stone says. "The whole country is starving, and we ate it smoked on the beach in Mog."

"Drank a few cold ones too," says Ademar with a sidelong glance at Deuce, as if to evoke a memory only they share.

Deuce hasn't smiled in a long time, maybe months, but he smiles at their secret, stolen intimacy in Somalia that December night by the Indian Ocean in a war zone on the other side of the world. "I remember," he says. "A million miles from Christmas."

Ademar squeezes Deuce's hand, breaks the silence. "So, Cap, you said there's something you have to tell us. Something you saw on the ride in?"

"Right," Stone says. "Running low on fuel north of your territory, New Mexico near Truth or Consequences. The Firehawk is a beast—big gas tank, long legs for extended fire-fighting, a belly that holds a thousand gallons of water. We refueled a bunch of times on the way down from Minnesota, and we knew the drill. Jesus, those fucking airfields, crawling with all kinds of trouble. A functional chopper was a magnet."

"Every stop was like Bakaara Market in Mog during the war," Charlie says. "*Black Hawk Down* on steroids, only no Seals for backup if we screwed the pooch."

"Anyway," Stone says, "we're circling the little airport in Truth or Consequences, found a QAV-1 tanker. Seemed clear. Set her down. There's a few bodies around the truck, the usual, but no incoming. Quiet. Eerily quiet. Truck battery is dead, auxiliary too, so we're using a hand pump. Still nothing unusual. We're counting our blessings when all hell breaks loose. Must have been twenty scavengers sprinting at us across the tarmac. Tell you the truth, looked like a bunch of cavemen. I almost had to laugh, until one of them chucked a spear—a fucking spear! The others were yelling and swinging homemade slingshots, slingshots hurling two-inch steel ball bearings. Spooky. Some real medieval shit. I make a run for the chopper, and Charlie is taking them down like dead grass with the SAW, that beast of a machine gun we took from the Stillwater National Guard post near Minneapolis. She cranks up, Charlie jumps in, and we're airborne. No harm, no foul."

"Okay," Ademar says. "I know your stories, Cap. Enough with the color. What's your point?"

"Had a little fun with it. Circled over them and dropped the whole load of water. Probably their first shower since the Fall."

Arwen giggles. "That's funny, Cap."

"What's life, baby girl, if you can't have a little fun in the apocalypse?"

"And?" Deuce says.

"After the shenanigans, we head to the border, over the Guadalupes, and we stopped laughing, real quick. There was a herd of these cavemen, maybe fifty, jogging—yeah, jogging—this way."

"They'll get religion at our outpost near there, the one at Bezos's old launch facility in Culberson County," Ademar says. "I'll hit our guys on the short wave."

"I don't think they'll go anywhere near there," Cap says. "Except maybe for a diversion. Hard to tell."

"Why not?" Ademar says. "It's not like they have any battlefield intel."

"That's where you're wrong," Cap says. "That herd was being driven by a bunch of women on horseback, maybe twenty of them. Women with real weapons, driving them with bullwhips like cattle. I think they're heading this way. And they're using those scavengers as cannon fodder."

"The Sisterhood," Ademar says.

"Exactly," Stone says.

"But that's not enough to come right at us," Deuce says. "What are those she-devils up to?"

"Shit, they could be anywhere by morning," Ademar says. "We'll saddle up and see what's what."

"Chopper?" Charlie asks.

"Can't risk it," Ademar replies. "We've got Stingers. Sisterhood might too. Only horses. But we'll go in heavy, plenty of guns."

"Just like old times, Ranger," says Charlie, who called Ademar Ranger during the days in Somalia when he was her translator and she was an Army Ranger.

"Sounds like fun," Arwen says. "Can I come?"

"No way, Arwen," Ademar says. "You're staying put with Star."

The defenders of the Long Now, a small, well-armed contingent of forty Free People, see dust on the horizon, orange dust in the rising sun, before the herd gallops down the hill like stampeding buffalo. One innocent, oblivious chime rings from the mythic timepiece, the Clock of the Long Now that Bezos buried deep in a mountain across Highway 54 from his Blue Origin rocket launch site outside Van Horn. Designed to last ten thousand years, the mechanical monument has survived long after the shrewd billionaire catapulted himself and his family into space a few days after the Fall. Their rocket floats aimlessly somewhere in space, out of fuel and full of dead rich people. The conceits of presumed immortality yielding to the cold reality of the apocalypse. Other than the daily chime, a bygone pentimento to time in a world where time is measured by the Terra-Algorithm of the sun and the seasons, the mountain in which the clock is buried serves as a crow's nest for the Free People near their northern border.

A sniper armed with an M24 and long-range scope sights in on the two lead marauders and takes them down in succession. They are easy head shots from two hundred yards, and the 7.62 mm round racing through the thin desert air at 2,500 feet per second nearly decapitates them. Both bend sharply backward with the impact, but their momentum propels them forward like cartwheeling wooden puppets, stone-cold dead before they slam into a towering yucca cactus. The others stop, cowering behind whatever protection they can find. But tumbleweeds don't offer much in the way of a shield, nothing against a high-caliber load, and the sniper drops two more. Ademar, Charlie, Stone, and fifteen other Free People watch from a safe distance atop a hill about a half mile away.

"Nice sharpshooting," Stone crackles over a walkie-talkie to the others. "They're just short of the mines. Turkey and dressing if they keep coming, with plenty of gravy."

Ademar watches closely through the binoculars. "You won't fucking believe it," she says and hands the binoculars to Stone. Behind the herd, in full body armor on horseback, a group of Sisterhood warriors are galloping through the supine scavengers whipping them mercilessly. They leap up and run toward the compound, straight into the minefield, and the high explosives pop them like overripe melons. Ademar and her crew hear the hollow thump of 60 mm mortar shells from the Blue Origin compound about the time the ordnance hits the would-be marauders. Not much left standing, except for the Sisterhood forces galloping north hellbent for leather.

"How many of those bitches?" Ademar asks Stone.

"Strange," he replies. "I count fifteen."

"Right?" Charlie says. "We saw twenty of them from the chopper."

"Shit!" Stone shouts. "This was a diversion. OIT. Old Indian trick. What the hell are they up to?"

"Arwen," Ademar says. "Let's ride!"

Arwen floats aimlessly in the stock tank a few miles from the Dell City headquarters, the wispy strands of red grown-up hair in places other than her head a welcome reminder of advancing womanhood. Star snaps happily at water bubbles as she dogpaddles, of course, around Arwen in the tank. Her horse, Boquillas, Bo, grazes nearby. Arwen knew she shouldn't disobey Ademar and leave the compound. But teenagers will be teenagers, and Arwen could be a particularly headstrong one. *Besides*, Arwen thought as she slid the .30-30 into the leather scabbard at the barn, *the tank is only a few miles away from the compound.*

Bo snickers. Arwen looks up, and Star freezes, then is over the side of the tank in a second and in full fighting mode, ears back, hair up, fangs bared. Five horse heads stretch over the edge of the tank for a drink, atop them five Sisterhood warriors. One of them draws a pistol as Star leaps at her. "Don't waste your ammo," one says and whips Star bloody until she can only lie on the ground in full submission. The Sister walks her horse slowly to Star, still growling on her back, and casually tramples the dog until she hears the sharp crack of a foreleg. "Fucking dog," she says.

Arwen leaps from the tank and sprints toward Bo and the .30-30. Another Sister intercepts Arwen, and her comrades laugh. Arwen, defeated, five against one, stands buck naked and dripping wet between the five horses surrounding her.

"Pretty, ain't she?" says one of the Sisters.

"And clean as a little whistle," says another. "Good enough to eat."

"Get your mind off the pussy," the leader says. "Mother wants her fresh."

"C'mon," whines another Sister. "Just a taste?"

The lead Sister raises her arm and comes down on her with a fierce lash of the whip. "Dress Red and tie her up. We need to hightail it outta here." Laugh. "Excuse the pun."

Ademar, Stone, and Charlie gallop into the Dell City compound, horses wet with sweat from a hard day's ride. Nothing seems awry, until Ademar dismounts and checks the barn. "Where's Arwen, Bo, Star?" Ademar whistles, and Bo, empty saddle, trots around the corral and toward the barn. "God dammit!" Ademar shouts.

Her deadgrass-colored coat caked with blood, Star limps up slowly, barely able to walk, one leg up and bent at a right angle where it shouldn't be. Star, who knows she failed in the only task that mattered that day, can't look Ademar in the eyes. Ademar knows it when their eyes finally meet.

"They have Arwen," she says.

CHAPTER 13

AFTER THE FALL

The small band of Sisterhood warriors ride hard from the farm in Dell City to their compound deep in the Gila Wilderness of southern New Mexico. Arwen, a bloody mess of cactus gouges and chapped skin, rides strapped to the withers of a horse for the entire two hundred miles over rough terrain. Brief respites for food or water are the only opportunities Arwen has to relieve herself, and she has to go where she is tied to the horse when the urge strikes between stops. The acidity and filth of that inconvenience raises blisters between her legs that pop, ooze, and sting. Her wrists and ankles are bound with rawhide, soaking wet since they tied her up right out of the water tank in Dell City. They have shrunk in the dry high desert heat, cutting into her ankles and wrists with every mile. Stinging flies feast on the caked blood and pus that oozes from the wounds. At least they dress her for the ride, which spares her skin from the desert sun.

Arwen blocks out everything during the ordeal, meditating with circular breaths as the Lakota shaman White Eagle taught her during a sweat lodge ceremony in South Dakota a few years before the Fall. In through her nose, out through her mouth, mile after mile. Empty mind, full heart—full with the tiny bit of joy in knowing Star and Bo survived, and in the iron certainty that Ademar would not let this stand. 52 Blue comes to her during the journey, not some kind of hallucination but a true, indelible psychic connection. The whale's empathy for the young girl is like a mother's fierce love and overwhelming sadness for her child. It is a living manifestation of the Terra-Algorithm, the connectivity of the universe, Carl Jung's collective unconscious, all of which Arwen has come to understand through dreams and such inexplicable encounters as the one with the rattlesnake under the pecan tree. The clicks and hums of the giant blue whale soothe her almost as much as the very real feeling she experienced of cool ocean streaming over the whale arcing through the water on her way south.

The Sisterhood scouts stop just outside the main gate at their headquarters in what was once Our Lady of Guadalupe Monastery at the base of the Pinos Altos Mountain in the Southern Rockies of New Mexico. The irony of radicalized women warriors occupying a compound once used as a monastic retreat for Benedictine monks is lost on no one who gives it any thought, least of all the skeletons of several former occupants hanging by chains from the eaves of the four-story adobe bell tower. They were not the unlucky ones. The Sisterhood keeps dozens of the Monks alive and healthy for breeding and sport.

"Halt! Who goes there?" shouts one of the guards on the wall of the monastery.

"Who the fuck do you think?" the leader of the scouts shouts back. "Open the gate, you dumb cunt!"

"Look who's talking," Arwen says loud enough for the scouts to hear.

The scout on the horse with Arwen grabs a handful of her red hair and yanks hard enough to tear out a few strands.

"Nobody asked you, little one," she says. "You'll learn to keep quiet. By God, you'll learn fast."

If it hurts, and it does, Arwen does not give the Sister the pleasure of a whimper. Arwen doesn't whimper. The Free People of West Texas don't whimper. The Lawses and the Zarkans never bend the knee.

The reinforced wooden gate opens, and the five Sisterhood scouts gallop in with their prize, reining in the quarter horses to a sharp stop amid a rising cloud of dust. The ties that secure Arwen to the horse are cut, and she drops to the ground with a dull thud. Arwen scrambles to her feet, teeth clenched, fists balled and ready to fight. Arwen, twelve years old and alone against impossible odds. One of the scouts lashes her with a bullwhip violently enough to rip her shirt. A thin line surfaces, red, then almost black as it soaks into the faded blue denim.

"Is that all you got?" Arwen asks.

The scout snickers. Two Sisters, enormous women, spears crossed, guard a door in an adjacent wall. The door creaks open, and all heads turn as a figure emerges, almost floating, from the shadow. Mother.

"Well, well, well," says Mother, tossing her long braid back so Arwen can see on the shaved side of her head the tattoo of the praying mantis devouring her mate. "Arwen Laws, I presume. Good work, ladies."

Arwen is reminded of an image she saw in an old magazine of a Soviet female weightlifter, chunky and squat, square head, enormous hands and bulging calves below what looks like some kind of comical Romanesque toga. Arwen suppresses a laugh, but a smile squeezes out. Mother shuffles with a duck-footed walk to within an inch of Arwen and bends to touch foreheads. She inhales deeply, closing her eyes as if to savor the smell of something somehow nostalgic; leans back slightly; winks at her acolytes in the courtyard; then, with full force, slams her head into Arwen's temple. The young girl crumples to the ground unconscious.

"Clean her up," Mother commands everyone within earshot. "Food and water. Lock her in my adjoining room. Anyone who touches her will answer to me. Got it?"

"Yes, Mother!" they shout in unison.

Mother shuffles back to her quarters, pulls the heavy door behind her, and crumples to the ground. A silent scream of remembrance and agony pulses through every fiber of her being, fighting its way out for a release that will never come. Mother thinks she is past it, past the pain, past the sadness, hardened to anything resembling remorse or guilt. But the sight of Arwen, her fierce will to live and adolescent smell, triggers a memory of a time when life seemed normal compared to the hell of this apocalypse. She rocks back and forth, keening in silence for the death of Feather, the sweet Indigenous girl she was before the rape, before her daughter's death, before the Fall. What would the Sisters think if they saw her: exposed, weak, vulnerable? The silent scream, once out, cannot be pulled back in, like a breach in a dike that spreads inch by inch regardless of how many desperate fingers are thrust into it. Mother struggles to her feet and stumbles to a wall safe in a closet. It is a road to a past that she dares not open. But open it she does and pulls out a dusty scrapbook, titled *Little Feather*.

Mother was a mother before she was Mother. She was the daughter of a Lakota Sioux couple living on the Pine Ridge Reservation in South Dakota. It was a communal life tied irrevocably to the ebb and flow of the Terra-Algorithm. Simple and pure. If there was not enough food, the men would hunt for deer. The schoolhouse was a ramshackle one-room clapboard, cold in the winter and hot in the summer. But the young white instructor from Teach For America was a crackerjack determined the children would not fall behind in their

studies. Feather, Mother's given name, read far above her age
and liked nothing more than curling up by a fire with a book
of poetry, particularly Shakespeare's sonnets, which took her
to a world of fantasy far removed from Pine Ridge. Medical
care, adequate for stitching a wound or delivering a baby, was
as basic as it comes on a Native American reservation. What
the federal government could not provide through the Indian
Health Service was supplemented by White Eagle, the Lakota
Sioux shaman who had delivered Feather on a frigid winter
night when her mother could not make it over the icy roads
to the clinic. An immutable bond formed the moment White
Eagle teased Feather's little head from her mother's womb, and
she was like another daughter to him, until she disappeared
after the Fall.

A picture of White Eagle—young, handsome, strong,
with a jet-black braid halfway down his back, leaning over
Feather nursing on her mother's breast moments after birth—
barely sticks to the first page. Dried brown glue streaks peek
out from underneath the photograph where it doesn't hold
anymore. Mother smiles and thumbs through the next dozen
or so pages: Feather smiling with her first tooth, Feather
kneeling next to her first deer, Feather dressed to the nines
for her first dance at sixteen. Feather's father called her *princess*
that night and kissed her forehead as she walked out the
door. Mother stops. The smile melts away like sand under an
incoming tide. That was the night of the rape.

Mother opens her mouth to keen, but the pain is so deep
that not a sound comes out, like the frozen, silent moment of
pain and insanity depicted in Edvard Munch's painting *The
Scream*. A silent howl for everything she lost that night. The
pain is unbearable. She reaches into the safe for something she
swore never to use again, something like a sweat lodge that
surfaces and banishes trauma. Mother shakes two capsules
from a pill bottle—green on one end, white on the other—and

swallows them without water. She waits patiently until the hypnotic hum of the ibogaine begins to take effect. Extracted from the root of the iboga shrub in the rainforests of Central Africa, ibogaine is a powerful psychedelic used by progressive therapists before the Fall to help patients disassociate from such powerful trauma as war wounds or addiction. Mother lies down with the scrapbook on her chest as the drug takes hold. It is painful, like a parasite inside of her eating its way through every microfiber of her being until it finds the paralyzing trauma. The agony stops suddenly, like birth without the pain. She is able to revisit and process her past without the subsequent horror, devastation, and torment. Mother sees herself, sees Feather at sixteen obliterated by alcohol with the four white men from town tearing off her clothes. She feels the hands poking, twisting, holding her wrists and ankles. She sees the one with the big belly unclasp his huge belt buckle and drop his pants. She feels him enter her. She feels all four of them taking their turns and hears them laughing at "Pocahontas" as they walk away, leaving her crumpled and defiled on the cold, loamy earth behind a barn. Resurrecting that memory feels like childbirth, with the pain, but afterward all that's left is the elation of holding a baby. The therapeutic magic of ibogaine. Nine months later Little Feather was born, the only child Mother will ever have.

Mother feels better and sits up, thumbing through a few more pages to a photograph of Feather and White Eagle emerging from a sweat lodge ceremony, the only natural treatment that worked to help her process the rape. She looks through several pages of the scrapbook to the last page and a photograph of Little Feather at twelve smiling as wide as the Grand Canyon with a barrel-racing trophy in her hand. Mother glances through a window at an adjoining bathroom where two Sisters bathe Arwen and remembers exactly how it felt to be a mother washing a child. She feels the ibogaine parasite gnawing again and lies down. The hungry alien inside her slows down and stops. Feather is carrying Little Feather, burning with fever and racked with coughing spasms, out of a civilian hospital in Rapid City where a doctor turned her away because his Covid ward was full. The unquenched anger of radicalization against men, the fury that formed the foundation of the Sisterhood after the Fall, never eased after this moment. The drug leaves Mother by the grave of Little Feather. An image rises from the ground, and it is Arwen and a blue whale.

Arwen's harsh treatment at the hands of her captors has given way to what one could only be considered pampering: three meals a day, bathing, clean bandages for her wounds, and regular visits from Mother. Arwen hears the lock twist open on the door to the room adjoining Mother's quarters, and the leader of the Sisterhood steps in with a smile.

"Hello, Arwen," Mother says. "In the mood for a poem?"

"I can read," Arwen says.

"When I was your age," Mother says, "Shakespeare was one of my favorites. Do you know him?"

"Yes."

"Do you know his sonnets?"

"Some."

"This is number six:

> *Then let not winter's ragged hand deface*
> *In thee thy summer, ere thou be distilled:*
> *Make sweet some vial; treasure thou some place*
> *With beauty's treasure ere it be self-killed.*
> *That use is not forbidden usury;*
> *Which happies those that pay the willing loan;*
> *That's for thy self to breed another thee,*

Or ten times happier, be it ten for one;
Ten times thy self were happier than thou art,
If ten of thine ten times refigured thee:
Then what could death do if thou shouldst depart,
Leaving thee living in posterity?
Be not self-willed, for thou art much too fair
To be death's conquest and make worms thine heir.

"Do you understand?" Mother asks.

"No," replies Arwen, staring defiantly straight into Mother's eyes. "And I could care less."

"You will be with us forever, Arwen. You will bear children, my grandchildren. I am your *abuela* now, child. And that whale will be mine too."

"Whale?" asks Arwen, feigning ignorance. "What whale?"

"Don't play games with me, Arwen. You know exactly which whale. The one with all the answers to all the questions. But that's a matter for another time. Our task this morning, this fine Saturday morning, is to find you a breeding partner."

Mother takes Arwen's hand in a viselike grip, leading her out of the room and into the courtyard, where several hundred Sisters wait for the ceremonial walk to what for all intents and purposes is a bull ring. They all stop outside a door halfway to the ring and wait, except for a dozen Sisters who assume a running crouch in front of the closed portal. Arwen recalls a magazine article she read about the running of the bulls in Pamplona, Spain, in which the bravest, or most foolish, try to outrun fighting bulls on their way to the ring. Mother nods and the door swings open. Arwen expects the thundering hooves and the slashing horns of one-thousand-pound beasts. What she sees are eight naked men with scimitars secured tightly to their heads rush out of the door in a full sprint at the Sisters in front of them. Arwen has seen trapped animals with that combination of fear and rage in their eyes, but never a human. The Sisters in front of the human bulls take off down the cobblestone street leading to the ring. One trips on an uneven cobblestone and falls forward. She tries to scramble up, but not quickly enough to avoid a slashing scimitar that catches her low in the ribs with a dull thud. The human bulls, Sisterhood captives, are prepared for this moment like trained athletes, fed well, exercised, and pumped full of steroids so they resemble Greek gods. They are injected with cocaine to prepare them for this day and know that only the most savage of them has a chance to survive. With that knowledge, the one that has hooked a Sister drives the scimitar deep into her chest and, with the power of a real bull, tosses her over his shoulder. He has driven the scimitar through a lung and into her heart. Blood bubbles from her mouth, and she drops to the ground dead. The human bull turns, slashing madly from side to side. A Sister catapults herself over his shoulders, landing directly in front of him, then tears off toward the ring with the human bull in wild pursuit.

"Bravo!" the crowd of Sisters yells. "Olé!"

The runners sprint through the archway leading into the dirt ring, the human bulls in hot pursuit, and quickly slip to safety through open gates behind wooden barricades forming an inner circle around the small stadium. The bovine gladiators have been prepared for this moment, snorting and circling the ring, awaiting their *momento de la verdad*, their moment of truth. One of them, only one, will be spared and "put out to pasture" for breeding. If only they knew how that ended—tied to a bed, pumped full of Viagra, fucked silly for as long as they can perform, then castrated and buried alive— they might opt for death in the ring.

Mother and her senior Sisterhood acolytes sit on a raised dais cordoned off with blue velvet curtains from the rest of the crowd. They pick at dried fruit and nuts in bowls before them and drink from ornate goblets that the Benedictine monks once used as sacred chalices. Mother sits on a raised wooden throne so she appears taller than anyone near her. Arwen, stunned and speechless, sits on a smaller, similar seat, which until this moment has never been occupied.

"All but one will die," Mother says. "You decide."

"Decide what?" Arwen asks.

"Which one will be your breeder. Which one will produce your child and my grandchild."

"I'm not old enough," says Arwen, recovering her wits.

"You have bled," says Mother. "You are ready."

Astride a horse, a Sister, lance in hand like a picador in a real bullfight, gallops into the ring. She singles out one of the human bulls, who charges at the horse and hooks the beast's belly with a scimitar. The picador leans over the human bull, head down and neck exposed, digging the lance into bulging shoulder muscles. After several rounds of this, the human bull will no longer be able to hold up his head, and the matador will have a clean angle to thrust her sword into the small spot where it will sever his spine and pierce his heart. If it's a clean kill, the human bull will fall like a ragdoll face-first to the ground, dead.

Mother turns to Arwen. "Beautiful in a way, don't you think?" she says.

"No," says Arwen. "What happens to the horse?"

Mother chuckles. "Silly girl. The horse dies, and we eat him."

The banderillera struts into the ring. She holds in each hand a banderilla, small lances wrapped in colorful crepe paper that are thrust into the human bulls' shoulders to further weaken those muscles and enable the proper head position for the inevitable kill. The banderillera dances in front of the human bull until he charges. At the last possible moment, before he can hook her with a "horn," she raises on her toes, leans over the human bull, stabs both banderillas into his shoulders, and spins safely to the side. In an obscene way, it is an act of pure grace and athleticism, and the crowd erupts in applause. "Olé!"

A real bullfight unfolds in three acts, and if the picador and banderillero prepare the bull properly, it will end with the bull dead on the ground and the matador thrusting his hands triumphantly in the air as the crowd showers him with flowers before he takes the ears and tail as trophies. The Sisterhood believes in authenticity, and the crowd erupts in cheers for the final act of their Saturday distraction. The bullfighter walks into the ring, red cape in one hand, curved sword in the other. Sunlight reflects off the sequins of her outfit—a vest over a loose white chemise, pedal pushers, black hose, and black slippers with a neat bow on the top. She walks slowly, proudly, to Mother's side of the ring and bows deeply. Mother nods, and the matador turns to face the human bull, four banderillas hanging from his shoulders as blood drips into the sand. Unlike a one-thousand-pound bull bred to fight and die in the ring, the human bull is utterly, completely defeated and humiliated. No match for anything, welcoming death. He looks up at Mother with pleading eyes, and she turns to Arwen.

"This one?" she says.

Arwen stares defiantly into the distance and refuses to answer.

Mother, looking straight at Arwen, thrusts one hand forward, thumb down. The matador drapes the cape over a stick in her left hand, raises the sword over her head, and walks slowly to the human bull. She summons him with a wave of the cape, initiating a *paso de pecho*, one of the most elegant and dangerous of passes. A stumbling, awkward lunge at the matador is the best he can muster. The matador lowers the cape so the human bull fully exposes the base of his spine, and drives the sword so deep into him that the point comes out of his chest on the other side. The human bull—a carpenter from El Paso, a father with a wife and two children before the Fall— is dead before he hits the sand. The crowd, except for Arwen, jumps to its feet and cheers. The matador acknowledges them with a bow, pulls an Uncle Henry Hawkbill from her vest, jerks the dead carpenter's head from the sand, and chops off both ears and the only appendage on a man's body resembling a tail. She struts around the ring.

"Olé!"

She stops in front of Mother.

"Olé!"

She tosses the trophies up to Mother, where they land at Arwen's feet.

"Olé!"

Mother smiles. "Perhaps the next one will be more to your liking," she says to Arwen.

CHAPTER 14

AFTER THE FALL

Crouching like the mountain lion for which he is named, Mawiya, the Raramuri leader, and hundreds of his people gather at the gateway to the Copper Canyon near the remnants of Ciudad Creel in the northern Chihuahuan state of Mexico. It's a festive Sunday. Women in woven pastel skirts and white blouses squat in circles chatting while cherubic, round-faced children nurse or draw random designs in the sand at their mothers' feet. Men wearing serapes, jogging shorts, and handmade huaraches, sandals with thin soles from the treads of tires, swap tales of their latest long-distance runs and pass a clay jug of *tesgüino*, warm beer brewed from corn that is a sacred part of their spiritual lives. There have been many passes while they wait for the start of *Ralajipame*, a game not dissimilar to soccer in which participants advance with their feet a ball of madroño wood to a goal as far as twenty miles away. *Tesgüino* has a calming effect, like the cool breeze rustling the leaves of the towering ponderosa pines and madroño trees that provide shade for them. Mawiya and his top lieutenant, El Caballo Blanco, White Horse, who everyone calls Caba, each swig from the jug of corn beer and take their positions at the starting line for the game. Mawiya and Caba will compete with men far younger than them in a feat of stamina commonplace for them but suicidal for most humans in their sixties. It's as if they jumped up off the couch to run the Boston Marathon. The old friends could have been middle-aged men anywhere in the world before the Fall, sipping their favorite brew, swapping good-natured taunts, fibbing about the size of a trout they caught or a woman they loved and lost. Mawiya tightens the strip on his sandals and tosses the ball in the air before the other players. The game is on!

Life after the Fall has not changed much for the Raramuri, an ancient people whose roots go back centuries to the Mogollon Indians of the desert Southwest. Indigenous to West Texas and northern Mexico, they are one of the origin tribes of ancient civilization. The Fall is hardly their first existential challenge. The Raramuri, peaceful and agrarian, could be fierce warriors. They repulsed the avaricious Spanish conquistadors, who coveted the silver deep in the mountains of their territory and executed Chief Teporaca in 1653, and resisted conversion by Jesuit priests. Through it all, right up until this very moment as Mawiya and Caba prepare for the game of *Ralajipame*, they ran. Archaeologists, sociologists, and historians before the Fall studied the Raramuri and tried to uncover the genetic, emotional, or psychological markers that imbued these ancient people with a cellular gift for endurance. Alexander Shepherd, an American who founded in 1900 the Copper Canyon town of Batopilas, hired them to haul an upright piano almost two hundred miles, which they did in three days and jogged back. Neither Shepherd nor any of the science-based explorations cracked the code for how these brown, wispy, jerky-tough humans could run hundreds of miles through the arid desert mountains without rest. Arwen asked Mawiya about it once, and his response made more sense than the volumes of studies and articles.

"We run because we can," Mawiya replied. "Raramuri, the light-footed ones. We are born with it, just as the pecan nut is born with fruit, a fish with gills. Our connection to nature, to the greater world. Most peoples have lost what binds them to the earth, to every living thing. Those who have survived this change in the world, this Fall, are saved because they have rediscovered it. We didn't have to reclaim what was never lost."

It made sense to the young girl, who had experienced that profound linkage in her psychic connection to 52 Blue, but she didn't have the term: Terra-Algorithm. There is another term that applies to the phenomenon of the Raramuri and the unique purpose they—and other Indigenous people, like White Eagle's Origin Tribes of the Mountain West—have in the universe. Mathematicians who study chaos theory, which seeks to explain connections between seemingly random occurrences, refer to it as the *butterfly effect*. Meteorologist Edward Lorenz coined the term in the 1960s, reasoning that small changes in atmospheric conditions could have dramatic impacts on weather thousands of miles away, like carbon emissions in China triggering a chain of events that over time melt polar ice. It is as if there is a linear relationship between a small gust of air from the wing of a butterfly and something else on the other side of the world. As if a giant blue whale deep in the Pacific Ocean leaps from the water and a twelve-year-old redheaded girl in West Texas dreams about it. Or a grotesque contest in a makeshift New Mexico bull ring is countered in the calculus of the earth by a peaceful, centuries-old game of *Ralajipame*. That is why the Raramuri endure. They are the counterweight on the other end of the existential teeter-totter that maintains balance in the universe.

None of the competitors in the game of *Ralajipame* have cracked a sweat a few miles from the finish line, despite the hundred-degree temperature, the mile-and-a-half elevation, and the merciless sun. There have been a few good-natured dust-ups, followed by laughter and a hand. Mawiya and Caba, who have won their share of contests over the years, jog behind and, despite the stature of another victorious notch in their belts, flip the madroño-wood ball to one of the younger men when it rolls their way. *Korima*, unconditional giving, sharing, infuses Raramuri life. *Korima* is their word for love. One of the young men cradles the ball on his foot as he nears the victory line, but flips it to another just before he crosses it. *Korima*. The match ends with hugs, smiles, and a new set of instant legends to recount when they return. They pass a jug of *pinole*, an energy drink composed of roasted corn, milk, and raw sugar, and jog the twenty miles back home.

The sun has just fallen behind the craggy outcrops near Creel, and the golden splinters of light pierce the remnants of a day well spent in a pastime older, centuries older, than any of its participants. Mawiya and Caba stop at a stone water trough that runs from a wooden sluice in a pond uphill. Squabbling Mexican chickadees nagging at a single eared quetzal perch on the sluice and dip in the water. The drops they shake from feathers catch the final light of the day, bending it through prisms of yellow, blue, and red. Stained-glass perfection of the Terra-Algorithm, as precious and delicate as the Sagrada Familia in Barcelona or the Nasir al-Mulk Mosque in Shiraz. Dusk is a time of feeding in the high desert, and the birds, wary of a sneaky coyote or a surreptitious rattler, are airborne the moment Caba pulls the long rope to the sluice so gravity, which never sleeps, can carry water to the trough. Young ones dance the dance of impatient children around the two men as the trough fills, and chirp in delight when Mawiya throws large scoops of cool water at them. They all look up when Mawiya's wife opens the door to their house, a simple wooden structure built into a cave, and the earthy aroma of a stewpot full of beans and corn pours out. Five children, two Mawiya's and three Caba's, tumble into the house and alight like shining fireflies on a bench at a long madroño-wood table carved by one of their ancestors from a single tree. There is a connection between this table and the one in the great room at the house in Dell City shared by the Lawses and Zarkans, between all tables where humans through the centuries have gathered in fellowship to share a meal. The children fidget impatiently, no less frenetic than the chickadees perched moments earlier on the uphill water sluice, and dig their spoons into the steaming bowls of stew before they hit the table. Mawiya and Caba take theirs outside so they can savor their meal in the gloaming.

There is no formal police force or security barriers among the Raramuri, rather a system of shared vigilance that falls at times to one member or another. That responsibility has become more immediate since the Fall, bolstered by a network of concealed net traps encompassing villages and scooping up intruders. Up until now, the traps have ensnared only animals, which the Raramuri, almost entirely vegetarian, set free. But this night a fellow villager informs Mawiya and Caba that they have captured something unique.

"You must come," he tells them.

"Later," Mawiya says. "We're eating."

"It can't wait," he says.

"Why?" Caba asks.

"These are not animals," he replies. "Humans. Women— white women. Fighters."

The glow of the day falls from them like hot wax from a sputtering candle. They set their bowls down and jog after him for nearly a mile until they reach a stand of ponderosa pines where two Sisterhood warriors hang suspended and tangled in the netting of a rope trap twenty feet above the ground. The two women, not much older than Arwen, thrash like feral animals. They hiss, spit, and threaten the two men standing next to their spears that fell to the ground the moment the netting, triggered by a sapling, whipped them skyward. Their anger masks fear deeply embedded by the propaganda of the Sisterhood. Like an illness, violent radicalism in them runs as deep as in any ISIS or Proud Boys foot soldier before the Fall. Injustice, disenfranchisement, misogyny, and abuse, most pointedly mental and physical abuse in the coven of the Sisterhood, has transformed them from functionaries at an Austin nonprofit into guerilla warriors willing—at the drop of a hat—to sacrifice their lives to preserve and to dominate the philosophical and geographical territory Mother has branded into them as if they were Black Angus calves on the sprawling 6666 Ranch halfway between Lubbock and Wichita Falls.

Although Mawiya has not encountered the Sisterhood, Ademar has told him about them and the threat they pose to the alliance between the Raramuri, the Free People of West Texas, and the Origin Tribes of the Mountain West. Mawiya understands radicalism, not in the way that the talking heads and think tank automatons preached it on Sunday morning news shows before the Fall, but in the way of someone whose people have been subjugated and abused for centuries. The Raramuri have fought and died at the hands of conquistadors, Jesuits, and, in modern times, prospectors and drug cartels. But their goals are not revenge, simply preservation of a life that lives in harmony with the universe, the collective unconscious, the Terra-Algorithm. The Raramuri could be fierce warriors, even eco-terrorists, but they know when to lay down the sword. And Mawiya knows what to do with the brainwashed young women dangling twenty feet overhead.

"The poison is here," Mawiya says.

"We must kill them," Caba says.

"No."

"*Chingao, cabron*," Caba answers. "*Estas loco?*"

"No," Mawiya says. "I'm not crazy."

"Then what?" Caba says.

"What would you have us do?" Mawiya asks.

"Do we have a choice? You've heard the stories about the *Hermandad*. Enemies. Unredeemable."

"There is always a choice, *amigo*. One does not make peace with his friends."

"But . . ."

"*Ninguna cosa*."

"Nothing?"

"Cut them down. Tie their hands."

The one-mile jog back to the commune in Creel is nothing for Caba and Mawiya, who turns off his mind in a form of running meditation where every step is a sacred connection to the earth, to ancestors who can no longer run, and most of all to the natural calculus that connects human, animal, and plant. It is torture for the two women, who, despite their fighting trim, battle dehydration, hunger, and the altitude to keep up. But the exertion drains their anger, and they stagger into Creel thirsty, hungry, and, for the moment, absolutely compliant. Most of the village gathers around the women, bent over, panting, sweating, and scared. The cyanide capsule in the locket that every Sister wears dangles around their necks, but their bound hands prevent them from reaching it. Mawiya yanks the lockets from their necks and tosses the suicide pills into the fire. "You won't need this," he says.

Mawiya reaches into one of their pockets and pulls out a carefully folded and sealed packet of Kate McLeod moisturizer, forbidden by the Sisterhood and concealed by this Sister as a vestige of civilization and femininity. The Sisters are certain they face the slow, agonizing death that they have been brainwashed to believe waits for them at the hands of the Raramuri, or any of their enemies. They collapse to their knees, praying for a swift execution.

"These two women are not our enemies!" Mawiya shouts. "They are scared young women. They are our guests. Give them food and water. They will run, and they will heal. *Korima!*"

The next morning, Mawiya is awakened by the crackle of a short-wave transmission. It is Ademar.

"They have her," Ademar says.

"Who?" Mawiya asks.

"Arwen. Mother, the Sisterhood."

"How?"

"Come to Dell City. I'll explain everything in person. No telling who can hear this."

"We'll leave in the morning. Be there in a few days."

"How? It's three hundred miles."

"We'll run, Ademar," Mawiya says. "Of course."

CHAPTER 15

AFTER THE FALL

A demar and Deuce lie naked and entwined with each other and with the rumpled bedsheets in the darkest moment of a day in the high desert. Those few minutes before the glow of sunlight breaches the mountains ringing Dell City, when the stars seem just beyond her fingertips, are the holiest moments of Ademar's day. This is the time she feels closest to the deity, and to her husband, Deuce. Despite their ages and the compromises of aging, passion, particularly at this time of day, is more than a memory of youth. Ademar tucks in closer to Deuce, feeling his warm chest on her back with each breath. She is in that space between sleep and consciousness, but all of Deuce slumbers, except for the part of him that rises between her legs. She presses against him, and he nuzzles into the tender spot only he knows on her neck between her collarbone and the back of her ear. Ademar opens her legs to accommodate Deuce, but the dull thud of something on the front porch jolts them both awake, and the languid magic between them only seconds ago vanishes. They both hope it is nothing more threatening than a Mexican ground squirrel hopping onto the porch or a pistachio falling from a branch—innocent noises so commonplace before the Fall. But they know better.

In an instant, Ademar wraps herself in a red flannel shirt and grabs the .30-30 leaning against the headboard, while Deuce jumps into a pair of faded Levi's with a Glock 9 mm strapped to the belt. Star, broken leg almost fully healed, bounds from the bed. Ears back, chest hard to the floor as she creeps to the door, Star knows not to bark. But a muffled growl rumbles deep in her chest with every breath and reverberates like a war drum off the Mexican tile floor.

"Easy, girl," Deuce says. Ademar crouches next to the front door, rifle barrel forward as Deuce opens it to peek out, pistol first. Deuce bobs his head in and out of the door, as he was taught during summer counterterrorism maneuvers at Camp Buckner in the hills around West Point. Ademar flips a switch by the door, and floodlights burst into the darkness, revealing an eight-by-ten manila envelope and, for a brief moment, a small drone helicopter whirring into the inky blackness.

"Clear," Deuce says.

"What is it?" Ademar says.

"Special delivery," Deuce answers.

They sit across from each other on either side of the aged pecan-wood table in the great room of the adjoining homes. The manila envelope has the diabolical logo of the Sisterhood, a praying mantis devouring its mate during copulation, stamped in red wax over the flap. Ademar picks up the letter opener by its deer-antler handle and slides the blade through the wax. She shakes it to make sure there are no surprises, like a scorpion, and pulls out a single sheet of paper, a letter from Arwen.

Dear Abuela,

If there are any children left in this world, I am not one of them. Nobody, least of all a thirteen-year-old, should see what I have seen the past few weeks. There is evil all around me. Even though I pray five times a day facing east like you taught me, I don't feel God. I hope he hasn't abandoned me? I remember the letter you showed me, the one Abuelo Deuce sent to his abuela Marcie when he was at West Point, and the part where he tells her about a stained-glass window in the chapel with writing that says, Quis ut Deus? Who is like God? And her response to him, "There is only one God." I know that God. I feel him or her or they in our life on the farm, every time I wake up with Star curled around me, every time I mount Bo, every time we laugh at one of Cap's lame jokes. There's no laughter where I am now. And here there is only one God. Her name is Mother. She decides who lives and who dies, like a God. But I know she is not a real God. She is a devil.

I'm sorry that I disobeyed you that day y'all went north to scout what these people, they call themselves the Sisterhood, were up to. Please forgive me? With Star and Bo, I thought it would be safe to go for a dip in the tank. But it wasn't, and these four Sisters captured me. They strapped me to a horse and rode a lot of days to this fort. I think it's somewhere in the mountains of New Mexico. Mother will read this letter, and she says I can't tell you any more details about my location. These women, and they are all women except for some captured men they use for breeding and other things I don't want to remember, remind me of how you described your twin brother, Anil. I remember what you told me about how he sort of lost his mind—you used the word "radicalized"—and joined a terrorist group in the Middle East. You said it was because he was bullied and disrespected, and becoming a terrorist was his way to get revenge. How sad that he ended up killing himself and Uncle Tam, who all of you loved. What kind of revenge is that? I don't know all the details, but I think that's somehow what happened to Mother and the Sisters. I think they are all just normal women from all over the Southwest: Santa Fe, Las Cruces, Fort Worth, Amarillo, and even Marathon. What I wouldn't give right now for one of those big ol' chicken-fried steaks smothered in cream gravy from the 12 Gage Restaurant in Marathon, or just a stack of pancakes hot off the griddle in your kitchen. They feed me pretty well here, mostly vegetables and vitamins so I'll be what Mother calls "a good breeder." I know what it means, but you never quite filled in the blanks for me on how it happens and what it means for me. You talked about love and intimacy, but that's not what Mother has in mind. I think her daughter died of Covid, and I'm the replacement to give her a granddaughter. She is always pointing to one man or another, poor guys they captured and who are just waiting for death, and asks if I want this one or that one. I just stay quiet, and mostly she kills them in the most horrible ways. She says I can breed since I now have periods. That started after they captured me. That's another thing you didn't fill in the blanks on. I'm not blaming you. I know you would have when the time came.

The only bright spot comes when I sleep at night, and that whale, the one I told you about, visits me in my dreams. I know her name now, 52 Blue, and the whole story behind her, including the part about a scientist storing all that computer information inside her body. Mother also knows, and I suppose a lot of other people do too because of a newspaper article just before the Fall. Mother thinks that getting the computer stuff will make her the most powerful person in the world. I don't know about that! But I do know that 52 Blue could save me, and in a weird way I think that's why she has connected with me.

Mother is willing to swap me for what's inside 52 Blue, and she wants to meet at Matagorda Island in South Padre. Makes me smile when I remember that trip we all took there a bunch of years ago, even Cap, who kept trying to surf and yelled "Hang ten!" or "Cowabunga!" just before he fell off. Somehow 52 Blue knows about this, and, in my dreams, I see her swimming there. I'm afraid for her and what Mother will do if she gets 52 Blue. I don't trust Mother! You shouldn't either. But maybe you can work it all out if there is a meeting. I do trust you! And I know the families, Cap, Charlie, and White Eagle will know what to do at that meeting. That school y'all went to on the Hudson River taught you well, and Cap has some experience too. You know what I mean? I love you, Abuela.

Here's what Mother has to say about it:

Sure enjoying your granddaughter. Such a sweet, fresh young lady—perfect breeding stock for us. This meeting is your only hope to see her again. Contact me on short wave, 11.6–12.2 Mhz. Don't be stupid, Ademar. The whale for Arwen; no bullshit and no tricks.

—Mother

Ademar slams her fist on the table and slides the letter to Deuce. "That bitch!" she says. "She leaves us with no choice."

"Damn straight," Deuce says. "They'll have the advantage of geography, but we have the experience. How many firefights between us?"

"What are you saying?"

"I'm saying we be smart. Plan for the worst and hope for the best."

"How?" Ademar says.

"First, get on the radio and confirm the meeting," Deuce says. "Then marshal our forces for a meeting here. Two West Point graduates, three Army Rangers, warriors from Africa and the Lakota Nation—plenty of firepower. We ought to be able to come up with a plan. And our ace in the hole: the Raramuri."

"Affirmative," Ademar says.

CHAPTER 16

AFTER THE FALL

As with the Raramuri and other Indigenous people after the Fall, life is not that different for White Eagle and the Lakota Sioux on what was essentially an internment camp in the Badlands of South Dakota. But after the great realignment of civilization, there were two major transformations on the Pine Ridge Reservation, a swath of grassland and granite spires the size of Rhode Island. First, it is no longer a sty for some of the poorest, sickest, and least-educated Americans, a forgotten corner of a nation where women were two and a half times more likely to be raped than anywhere else in the country. Second, it has become a melting pot after the Fall for Native Americans regardless of their tribal affiliation. The Fall enabled what centuries of warfare, negotiation, *mordida*, and advocacy could not: unification in one place under one banner of hundreds of Sioux, Comanche, Nez Perce, Navajo, and Apache. Nothing came close, except perhaps those few months during 1866 in Wyoming's Powder River Valley when the legendary Lakota Sioux chief Red Cloud and the young warrior Crazy Horse allied with the Cheyenne and the

Arapaho in a victorious battle to defend their land against the US Cavalry in its bloody campaign to open new territory for settlers and gold miners. Pine Ridge is no longer a reservation. It is home to the Origin Tribes of the Mountain West.

They are led by the mythical Lakota Sioux shaman White Cloud, who has lived, hunted, ranched, and farmed in unison with the Terra-Algorithm on the same plot of land for ninety years. His compound is largely unchanged, except for the addition of several comfortable wooden homes for his extended family, corrals, and an immense barn housing a stable of fine ponies. The houses are different insofar as the families that occupy them are different: Black, Muslim, and Somali in one; white Jewish and American in the other. The two families have much in common, most recently their escape from the chaos of Minneapolis as civilization unraveled to find refuge on Pine Ridge with their old friend White Eagle, who decades ago had rescued them from near death at the hands of white supremacists in the depths of a slot canyon. That bond was cemented during a Sun Dance that cleansed Charlie Christmas of the demons from his past who haunted him since the trauma of the Somali war and the flight to America. Prometheus Stone, the former Army captain, left the battlefields behind for a rabbi's pulpit, but not his appreciation for ironic humor that lessened many a soldier's load on heavy missions in Africa, the Balkans, and the Middle East. Stone smiles and shakes his head every time he thinks of what he considers his extended family: Jews, Muslims, Native Americans. *Oy vey! Salaam Alaikum! Atanikili!* In an insoluble alliance with the Free People of West Texas and the Raramuri, White Eagle and his people hold the western flank against the hounds of the apocalypse.

Hundreds of them are camped near Wounded Knee Creek, the site of a massacre in 1890 under a hail of bullets from the US Seventh Cavalry and a flashpoint for violence eighty years later between the American Indian Movement and law enforcement. Hewing to eons of traditions that have preserved their sacred bond to the land and to the spirits, the Lakota gather for a few weeks to celebrate the *Wiwanki Wachipi*, the Summer Sun Dance. This is a festive time for ceremony, feasting, crafting, dancing and communal bonding, but in the time since the Fall it has provided a pause in the cycles of their lives to assess the strategic landscape. Like most important parleys, the consultations take place in a sweat lodge, where men—and increasingly so since the Fall, women—gather under animal hides propped up with willow saplings and heated by stones from an open fire to a temperature well in excess of one hundred degrees. The *Inipi*, as it is called, is akin to a New Year's Eve sauna in Finland, where Fins gather to purify themselves for the challenges ahead over the next twelve months.

White Eagle; his wife, Red Thunder; Charlie Christmas; and Stone arise at dawn for a private session in the sweat lodge to mull over their options given the short-wave message from Ademar the previous night about the abduction of Arwen and her proposal for a war council at Rancho Seco outside Dell City. They sit around the heated stones that Red Thunder moved one by one with wooden tongs from a fire that has smoldered throughout the chill of a South Dakota night. It is a somber moment. Silence prevails, except for the slow drip of sweat pattering the tarp underneath and the hiss of steam rising from the water White Eagle splatters across the rocks with a hand-carved wooden ladle handed down through generations of his family. Stone laughs.

"What?" White Eagle asks.

"Nothing," Stone replies.

"Come on, Cap," says Charlie, coaxing the kind of Stone-ism from his old friend that has eased the tensions of many soldiers trying to reconcile their fates to the destiny of battle.

"A *shvitz*," Stone replies.

"Schlitz?" Red Thunder says with a chuckle. "You men are always ten minutes from the next cold one."

"No," Stone says. "*Shvitz.*" And a second time for emphasis: "*Shvitz*," emphasis on the *V.*

"Please, learned rabbi, let us in on the humor," says White Eagle.

"No disrespect intended," Stone says.

"None will be taken," White Eagle replies.

"We're like a bunch of old Hasids, Orthodox Jews, sweating our asses off in a Brooklyn bathhouse and kibitzing in Yiddish over a Talmudic interpretation."

Like most Stone-isms, this one is slightly off the mark. They all laugh anyway because his malapropisms of humor, combined with his boyish humility, even at the distinctly un-boyish age of seventy-two, constitutes the essence of why they feel such affection for him. That, and his heart: the heart of a true warrior. He is the reincarnation of Judas Maccabeus, the Jewish warrior-priest who led the revolt against the Seleucid ruler Antiochus before the birth of Christ.

"Not bad, huh?" Stone asks.

"Lame, as usual," Charlie replies. "Love you anyway."

"Indeed," Red Thunder says.

White Eagle chuckles, nods his head in agreement, and brushes the waist-length braid from his chest to the back of his neck. "Indeed. Now to the matter at hand. Our child, our Arwen." The mirth that hovered over them only a few seconds before evaporates like water on scalding-hot granite stones.

"We know the Sisterhood, and their Mother," White Eagle says. "I know this whale. I have seen her in visions. We are living in an allegory, and this creature is the messenger. We will go to Ademar. We will help rescue Arwen. We will see this whale. It is written."

Three days later they begin a journey of a thousand miles.

Twenty-five warriors, men and women of all ages representing the five tribes, sit astride horses in a straight line just after dawn. Dust from nervous hooves floats in the air. The distinct smell of horse and human hangs on the dust, translucent, yellow like onions in hot oil through the crisp morning light of a new sun. Stone—the battlefield Stone, not the affable officer of comic relief—reins in hand, walks his horse slowly to the end of the line.

"The smell of war in the morning," he says to nobody in particular, although Charlie and their two sons, Amiir and Noah, hear him clearly.

Stone pulls them aside. "Stay close. Don't be foolish. Strength and honor."

"*Inshallah*," Charlie says. *God willing.*

Horses are the only available transport since there is no heavy lift military equipment to accommodate the numbers, and even if there was, diesel fuel and avgas are almost nonexistent. If they push the horses, White Eagle figures the journey to Dell City will take two weeks—straight south through the Great Plains into Nebraska, across the Platte River west of Ogallala, through a sliver of southern Colorado between Kit Carson and Pritchett, and weaving to Ademar's compound on Rancho Seco through Amarillo, Portales, Roswell, and the Guadalupe Mountains. Stone and Charlie know war, but scant few, except for the old timers among the Sioux, Apache, Nez Perce, and Comanche, have felt the cold rush of adrenaline on a battlefield at dawn, or the waiting for it. War is not like the Netflix series most of them cut their teeth on. Truth be known, it's mostly hurry up and slow down, with lousy meals and little sleep in between. Then the fury, the death, the smell.

There are two warriors missing and a space between horses for them. A single drumbeat pierces the air, the deep, sonorous sound of a wooden stick striking an elk hide stretched tight across a hollow pine stump. White Eagle and Red Thunder, heads down in an act of humility before their warriors, some of whom may give their lives in the coming weeks, walk slowly to the front of the line. They are the only ones in the traditional dress of a warrior, White Eagle stripped to the waist in a pair of buckskin pants and beaded moccasins. A single eagle feather dangles by a strip of rawhide from his long braid, a razor-sharp tomahawk hangs from his belt, and an AR-15 rides in the leather scabbard on his saddle next to a battle lance with a polished wood staff and a notched steel point. Even at ninety, not a figure anyone would want to encounter in a dark alley, let alone across a battle line in the high desert of West Texas. Red Thunder's buckskin skirt, with enough room around the waist to conceal a Glock 9 mm, hangs below her knees, and an MK3 commando knife hangs from her belt. Hoping for the best, planning for the worst. They have painted yellow circles around their horses' eyes and noses for keen sight and a strong sense of smell, blue arrow points on their necks for victory, yellow arrowheads on all four hooves for speed, and red handprints on their shoulders for revenge.

Crossing the Great Plains and high desert on horseback in August is a hard mistress. But they are committed to her and determined to make the union work. They have no choice. One gift in the dowry of their epic journey, and one of the few plusses of the Fall, is the reversal of climate change in the absence of carbon emissions. The skies were never bluer, the streams are crystal clear and potable, game is plentiful, and violent weather, except for afternoon rainstorms, is almost nonexistent. Even the buffalo, restricted to federal reserves and largely protected from hunters in the year preceding the apocalypse, roam the High Plains in numbers not seen since before white settlers with their long rifles decimated them for skins, leaving the noble behemoths nothing but decaying corpses for coyotes and vultures. This was one of the many indignities heaped on the Indigenous people, who relied on bison meat to sustain them over long winters and thick coats to hold off the bone-cold wind. Beyond sustenance and warmth, the bison is a symbol of abundance, hope, bravery, kindness, strength, and respect for the American Indian, none more so than the scarce and mythic white buffalo. Legend has it that the white buffalo spirit walks a sacred path, knowing the planet is a holy space and a living creature. The Indigenous people of Alaska and Arctic lands, the Eskimos, hold the whale in similar esteem. And without being able to articulate it, Arwen tapped into the same connection with 52 Blue. This entire natural equation, this inexplicable calculus of the universe, is the essence of the Terra-Algorithm.

That is why White Eagle holds up his hand to halt the expeditionary force one day's ride from the Platte River in southern Nebraska when a lone white buffalo crests a nearby hill, his massive body nearly blocking the entire waning sun and casting a long shadow that almost touches the forehooves of his horse. He dismounts, kneels, and recites a prayer generations of his predecessors have chanted for this creature.

"O great spirit whose voice I hear in the winds, whose breath gives life to the world, hear me. I come to you as one of your many children. I am small and weak. I need your strength and your wisdom. May I walk in beauty. May my eyes ever behold the purple sunset. Make my hands respect the things you have made, and my ears sharp to hear your voice. Make me wise so I may know the things you have taught your children, the lessons that you have hidden in every leaf and rock. Make me strong, not to be superior to my brothers, but to fight my greatest enemy: myself. Make me ever ready to come to you with straight eyes, so that when life fades as with the fading sunset, my spirit will come to you without shame."

His supplication touches every rider, as deeply in those raised on the legend as in those who kneel to Allah, Jesus, or Yahweh.

They reach the Platte River with about an hour of light remaining. Wide and nearly bottomless, in some places one mile across and fifteen feet deep, it surges with bone-chilling waters from runoff that began as raindrops and snowflakes on the Continental Divide hundreds of miles away in the Rocky Mountains. With this perilous passage in mind, White Eagle sent an advance party ahead the previous day to scout for a manageable crossing.

"How does it look?" White Eagle asks one of the scouts as the whole party gathers on the north bank of what, by any measure, would be a formidable four-hundred-foot crossing point, with an island in the middle.

"About as good as it gets," answers the scout, pointing to a nest of thunderclouds forming in the distance and closing quickly on a building wind. "And it's not likely to get any better."

"Perhaps we should camp here for the night and try tomorrow," White Cloud says. "Hope for a small storm tonight and a dry day tomorrow."

"No," Stone says. "Only fools predict the weather. And I think we're being followed. Saw some tracks this afternoon. At least five riders. Two of them heavy, maybe weapons, deep prints. They won't make it here until dark. Damn sure won't try it at night. We get to the other side today, river protects our flank."

"Where'd you learn that trick?" Charlie asks.

"Not at West Point," Stone says with a smile. "Don't tell Ademar or Deuce I said that."

"But where to cross?" asks White Eagle.

"There," replies a scout, pointing to the island just as the white buffalo steps from behind a clump of bushes, ambles into the water, and walks to the other side across a sandbar a few feet below the surface.

"*Atanikili*," says White Cloud. *Awesome.*

Following the bison's lead, they make the passage without

incident. The skies open up once they are safely across, and within an hour the Platte is a raging, completely unnavigable brown torrent of hydraulics, eddies, and massive standing waves. It's no better in the morning, although the rain has subsided to a light drizzle. As usual, Stone is one of the first ones out of his tent at dawn, as much out of habit as out of the biological calling of a seventy-year-old bladder. White Eagle, standing by the river's edge to relieve himself, has almost two decades on Stone and waves him over.

"There," says White Eagle, pointing across what is now easily a half mile of water. "You were right, my friend."

Stone takes no satisfaction, never in matters of combat, when he follows the line of White Eagle's finger across the river to three Sisterhood warriors and two men. It would not be an easy shot with a sniper rifle, but not unheard of for many of the skilled marksmen with whom Stone served in the military, or Ademar in her prime. But Stone can see through his binoculars they carry only handguns, unsighted rifles, and spears, rendering the Lakota chief and the rabbi impossible targets, for now.

"They'll move fast. Small group," Stone says. "May have a day on them. We have the numbers if they catch up."

"Never underestimate the coyote," says White Eagle. "He is clever. Relentless."

Like young men everywhere, Noah and Amiir don't always ride with the pack. They drift away for hours at a time to chat about nothing in particular: life before the Fall, football, girls, movies, rap musicians, the intense pleasure of a chocolate milkshake from Sonic. They play a game where one picks a year and the other opines on the most consequential event during those twelve months. Such was their banter as they rode into the Llano Estacado, one of the largest tablelands in North America and, with its towering escarpments over deep gorges, the ideal stronghold for the Comanche until their final battles in the late nineteenth century at the hands of the US Cavalry. They are ten days into the journey, mostly uneventful except for thirst, hunger, and rattlesnakes, and the two young men have wandered more than a few miles from the main group to bullshit and to look for petroglyphs in a narrow canyon north of what was once the small town of Hope, New Mexico.

"2024?" says Amiir, launching their favorite pastime to take their minds off the heat and the wind.

"Easy," says Noah. "Arch Manning wins the first of his two national championships at UT. 2026?" he shoots back.

"Hmmm," Amiir ponders. "I'll go with Speaker of the House Kevin McCarthy having gender reassignment surgery."

"That was a thing?" Noah asks.

"Don't you read the newspaper, bra?" Amiir snaps back. "2030?"

"Dune 7, dude," Noah answers in a split second. "No question."

"Right," Amiir agrees. "Duncan Idaho lives!"

"And rules!" Noah says.

"I must not fear. Fear is the mind killer, the little death that brings total obliteration," says Amiir, quoting one of the iconic sayings from the movie.

"I will face my fear, permit it to pass over me and through me," says Noah, finishing the quote. "And when it has gone past, I will turn the inner eye to see its path. Where the fear has gone, there will be nothing. Only I will remain."

Deep in their game, the two friends laugh and start to bump fists, but freeze when they hear a sound completely out of place in the Llano. The metallic click of a pistol hammer engages behind a 9 mm bullet. Five riders emerge from the shadow of a cave: three Sisters and two men with the heavy beards and body art so common among biker gangs before the Fall. The larger of the men, Thor, has a swastika tattooed on one ripped bicep and a black Q, symbol of the far-right conspiracy group QAnon that plagued the nation before the Fall, on the other. His companion, Happy, has a macabre, cherry red, ear-to-ear smile tattooed around his mouth and a tourniquet pulled tight above the knee of a necrotic, stinking leg that can only be the work of a rattlesnake. The other three are Sisters, who have struck an uneasy alliance with the two men in exchange for their help capturing the war party headed for Dell City. It was an easy choice for Thor and Happy: "Cunt for muscle" is how Happy coined the arrangement. But he isn't feeling much like cunt three days into a snakebite that will take his leg, and likely his life. Thor doesn't really care; just means more for him.

"Looky here," says Thor, waving his gun back and forth between them. "What are you two niggers doin' in the desert?"

"You know exactly what we're doing," says Amiir.

"You're right," says one of the Sisters.

"Don't call me nigger," Noah says.

Thor walks his horse next to Noah, palms his pistol, and shoves it into the boy's nose, which snaps like a dry twig. Noah reels back but keeps his saddle, the words of the Dune quote still in his head: *I must not fear; fear is the mind killer* . . . Blood drips from his nose, down his chin, and onto his shirt drop by drop.

"Enough," says one of the Sisters. "We'll need them later."

Happy, clownish smile spread across his face for eternity, whines in pain when his horse jerks at the smell of blood. The two puncture wounds on his calf from the Mojave rattlesnake are crusted with dried blood and pus. The skin around them is jet black from calf to thigh, with bulbous black lumps the size of golf balls behind his knee. The ugly wound has split open from the poison and the heat of infection so that his leg looks like a diagram of a dissection for an anatomy book.

"Not looking so happy, Happy," says Thor, poking at the stinking leg with the butt of his spear.

"God damn, Thor!" Happy screams. "Do something. I'm dying here."

"Shut the fuck up," Thor says. "Don't be a pussy. That's what you get for pissing on a rattler."

"There's only one thing to do," a Sister says. "Take it off tonight."

"Hear that, Happy?" says Thor, turning to him and mimicking a sawing motion. "Something to look forward to tonight, *amigo* of mine."

A few miles away, Stone kicks dust to extinguish the fire where they have all gathered for the night. He and Charlie are accustomed to their sons riding in late, but not this late, and they have been searching the perimeter since sunset a few hours earlier.

"What?" asks White Eagle.

"We found their tracks a few miles away," Charlie says, "along with the tracks of five other riders, probably that crew from the river. Don't think we should have a fire."

"And blood," Stone says. "It's dark and it's dangerous. But we're going. Now."

Stone affixes a silencer and laser scope to his rifle, while Charlie chambers a round into his .30-30.

White Eagle tosses Charlie the tomahawk. "This may come in handy," he says.

It is not dissimilar to the Somali throwing sword Charlie wielded back in his homeland, and he stuffs the handle under his belt. "Thanks."

"If we're not back by morning," Stone says, "we're dead."

Stone and Charlie head out on foot under the cover of darkness, and within an hour they spot the small cooking fire in the distance at the mouth of a cave. "Showtime," Stone whispers.

"Back in the shit, again," Charlie replies. They have shared the heat of battle, and the moments just before, more times than they can remember. They are creaky warriors in their late seventies, but the years melt from them as adrenaline starts to kick in, and they are once again the Spartans of their youth who fought warlords in Somalia, ISIS terrorists in Kenya, and white supremacists in the American heartland. Rifles cradled in the crooks of their elbows, Stone and Charlie crawl halfway to the distant camp where their sons are held captive. They approach downwind, stopping just short of the point where the arc of light from the fire meets the darkness of the plain.

Thor jerks a bottle of sotol from Happy, who has been nursing it in preparation for the amputation. "That's enough," he says. "You're probably gonna be dead by dawn, and those Sisters need some lubrication to get in the mood for ol' Thor."

"Just kill me, please," Happy whines.

"Waste a bullet?" Thor says. "And alert those injuns over there where we are?"

"Stab me in the head, cut my throat," Happy pleads. "Anything. I can't stand it."

One of the Sisters draws a smoking, red-hot knife from the fire while the others gather what scant first-aid supplies they have for the gruesome operation. Noah and Amiir sit against the tree where they are tied, twisting in vain to break free from the rope. The Sisters stand over Happy, delirious with fever and half-drunk on sotol. One of the Sisters grabs Happy's leg, pulling it taught so the knife will pass through more easily, and Thor digs both knees into his shoulders, immobilizing the snakebit man and breaking his left collarbone with a sharp snap. Happy shivers in agony as the "surgeon" shoves a piece of wood between his teeth so he can bite down against the pain, and so he won't scream.

Stone motions for Charlie to work his way to the other side of the camp, then, for a brief second, flashes the boys with his laser scope. Amiir, no stranger to the weapons of war, recognizes immediately what it is. "Our guys," he whispers to Noah. "Stay chilly."

Stone gives Charlie a moment to crawl to the other side, then trains the laser on the bridge of Thor's nose just between his eyes. The night explodes. Everything happens at once. Stone pulls the trigger just as the knife digs into Happy's leg. The top of Thor's head pops off, and he falls forward over Happy's body. The Sisters look up, no idea what has happened since Stone's rifle was silenced. Nothing is quieter than a tomahawk, and the cartwheeling blade leaves Charlie's hand silently, embedding itself deep in the surgeon's face and killing her instantly. The other Sister leaps to her feet but drops instantly as two silenced bullets from Stone's AR-15 tattoo her chest. Stone and Charlie emerge from the darkness like angels of death, while Noah and Amiir sit in stunned silence.

"Turkey shoot," Stone says.

"What do we do with this one," says Charlie, motioning to Happy writhing in pain on the ground with half his leg cut to the bone.

"I'll take care of it," Stone says. "Untie the boys."

"End it, please," Happy begs. "Don't leave me for the vultures and coyotes."

"Happy to oblige," says Stone, who jams the barrel into Happy's smile and pulls the trigger.

Stone and Charlie walk back to their camp in silence, but the boys can't stop chattering about what they just saw. Young men before the Fall might have been in shock from the trauma of their last six hours, but death and brutality have become familiar companions for the two boys, and they seem no more fazed than if they had just prevailed in a particularly lively online game of Battlefield V. Stone understands that for every soldier there is a first battle, and first kill, but he can't allow this moment to pass for them without context.

"There's no honor in exterminating vermin," Stone says. "They got exactly what they deserved. Could have gone a lot worse for you two. Breaks my heart to think about it. But there's a lesson here, always a lesson."

"We know," Noah says.

"We shouldn't have strayed so far away," says Amiir, completing the thought.

"Damn straight," Charlie says. "Reckless disregard."

"Enough," Stone says. "They get it."

Stone and Charlie walk into camp with arms around their sons' shoulders and exchange a glance with White Eagle that transcends the need for any explanation.

"Those five over there," says Stone, motioning his rifle toward the other camp, "won't be a problem anymore."

As the plains of the Llano Estacado give way to the high desert, a few days ride from Dell City, the group crests a hill above a small watering hole, and they ride there to camp for the night. Just before full dark, their old friend, the white buffalo, with a white buffalo calf, appears like a spirit above them on the hill. The adult buffalo lumbers to the pond, but the calf, unfamiliar with the smell of humans and horses, hesitates for a moment before kicking both rear hooves in the air and playfully scooting to the water. It is nothing short of a miracle—the entire journey has been something of a miracle—and, after the buffalos walk into the night, White Eagle acknowledges it.

"It matters not to whom you pray," White Eagle tells them. "Every people have their prophets. For us, the Lakota Sioux, it's the white buffalo.

"Long ago, the White Buffalo Calf Woman appeared to a hunter and promised to teach our tribe the secrets of the sweat lodge; the prayer pipe; the Sun Dance; naming, healing, and marriage ceremonies; and the vision quest. She magically changed into a white buffalo calf after bestowing those sacred rituals upon us, but, just before, she promised to return as a sign of peace amid war and confusion. What happened on this journey, and today, is no coincidence. It is the fulfillment of her prophecy."

They never see the white buffalo again, at least not as long as they live.

CHAPTER 17

AFTER THE FALL

There are nuances in the land of the midnight sun that Hannah Spencer, the marine biologist from suburban DC who pilfered the world's algorithms, did not anticipate. As a scientist, she prides herself in analysis, prediction, and preparation. But daylight around the clock on a small island in the Arctic Sea was not something she prepared for, particularly with a nine-year-old and a newborn. That's why she finds herself at three in the morning on an August day walking along the beach with her husband, Jeremiah; nine-year-old daughter, Azul; and newborn son, Jack. Needless to say, Jack is on her breast, again.

Life after the Fall in the Norwegian archipelago of Svalbard could not be more different from the high desert of West Texas, almost as if the environmentally conscious Norwegians knew all along that civilization would one day melt down. The Spencers live in an ultra-modern box—constructed of recycled materials with a water purification system, hydroponic garden, chickens, composting toilets, radiant floor heat fueled by methane from the sewage system, and solar—perched on a cliff above the sea. It is by no means spartan and would not be out of place, or particularly affordable, in the hippest neighborhoods of Brooklyn or San Francisco. Seafood is plentiful, either from a fisherman in the village or directly from the bay, and the family is the picture of health. Jack, red-cheeked and pinchably pudgy, and Azul, gamine of the sea with her stuffed whale Blue never out of reach, enjoy nothing more than playing on the beach while Jeremiah casts for char or wades after crustaceans. The bays are alive with lobster, oysters, and crab since the Fall and the restoration of normal, clean water teeming with aquatic vegetation. There is no Sisterhood, or radicalized people, although the local constable can be out of sorts without his coffee and pipe in the morning. The hospital can handle almost anything, from stitches and concussions to childbirth and chemotherapy, and there hasn't been a case of coronavirus since before the Fall. Community squabbles, nothing more than public drunkenness or rights to boat slips, are arbitrated by an elected town council. Humans are left to be humans, and it works.

They live in near-perfect harmony with the Terra-Algorithm.

But they are all acutely aware of the darkness that has consumed the earth, Hannah more than most, as well as her friends among the Samis, semi-nomadic Indigenous people who have inhabited Lapland for centuries and whose lives revolve around reindeer. There are those that claim Santa Claus is a Sami, and Azul is certain Erke, an octogenarian whose silver beard is as generous as his waistline, is Saint Nick. To his great delight, Azul calls him Mr. Claus, and each Christmas she climbs into his ample lap to whisper the gifts she hopes to find under the tree. And to Hannah's great delight, Erke has become a trusted advisor and friend, someone with the intellectual breadth and worldliness, gathered during his voyages from one end of the earth to the other, to understand what she has done.

Hannah is troubled, and he can sense the turbulence in her soul. The Nordic glow of the midnight sun casts a golden hue on the two of them during one of their heart-to-hearts on the beach in the sleepless hours before children awake and life surges into its daily routine.

"Tell me, Hannah," Erke says.

"Nothing," she replies.

"Don't bullshit a bullshitter," he says.

"Reindeershitter would be more accurate," she says.

"Okay, Hannah," he persists. "Tell me."

"Something you don't know."

"Plenty I don't know."

"Important."

"So little in these times is not."

"I did a crime just before the end times, a crime that my government, any government, would consider high treason," Hannah says. "Death sentence."

"Who is innocent?" Erke posits.

"Not a rhetorical matter," says Hannah.

"I killed a man," Erke says. "Hard to imagine, I know. Santa Claus the cutthroat. But I was not always like this. I was quick to anger, game for a fight. And he, well, as you say in America, 'dissed' me in the most insulting way. Not a unique story for a sailor. Below-deck card game on the high sea. Everyone drunk. He was a big man, German, not the most popular. It escalated, fists to knives. And I killed him. We threw him overboard. Never told the captain, and he didn't ask many questions. What's the saying? Dead men tell no tales. I dream about him sometimes."

"Dreams, huh?" Hannah says. "Mine ends with a dream."

"And how does it begin?"

Hannah turns away from Erke, toward the sea. She puts one finger under the elastic tie to adjust her ponytail, in the way women do sometimes to stall, to gather their thoughts, and flips it all forward over her head and back. She turns away from the sea, toward Erke, and twists her hair back into the tie. Hannah begins, and over the next hour, as Erke puffs on the long stem of his wood-and-reindeer-bone pipe, lays out the entire story of the undersea cables, the algorithms, and the whale. She leaves out no detail, not even the part where 52 Blue rescued Azul after she fell in the water.

"Almost unbelievable," he says.

"Believe it," Hannah replies. "There's more. And I'm struggling with it."

"More?" he questions.

"I dream about this whale almost every night. But not like a dream, like a connection, a communication. I'm a scientist—not supposed to believe in dreams, only data."

"Believe, Hannah," he replies. "We know there is a creator."

"I can," she says. "Especially now."

"Why now?"

"Now it's a three-way communication," she explains. "52 Blue, me, and a redheaded teenage girl in Far West Texas. Unreal, really. She has summoned the whale from the Arctic to the coast of Texas. I see the journey in my dreams. The girl is being held captive by a band of women, a vicious cult who want the whale. Well, what I put inside 52 Blue, to be more precise. Their leader thinks it will give her power over everything. And it would—it could.

"But not in the way she thinks. Let's walk. I'll explain."

As Hannah concludes her explanation, Jeremiah, Azul on his hand and Jack in his arms, greets them at the bottom of the wooden stairway leading to their house. Erke taps his pipe on a rock to clear the ashes. "You are a clever human," he says to Hannah.

"Mommy is?" Azul asks.

"Yes," Erke replies. "Mommy is."

CHAPTER 18

AFTER THE FALL

On a dry track in Pennsylvania during a windless spring day in May 2008, Winning Brew ran a blistering forty-four miles per hour, officially the fastest speed ever recorded by a horse. The Jamaican sprinter Usain Bolt holds the record for humans at almost twenty-eight miles per hour over one hundred meters. A world-class marathoner maintains a speed of twelve miles per hour for more than three hours during a twenty-six-mile race, while a better-than-average jogger might keep a speed of seven miles per hour. Mawiya, Caba, and the Raramuri plan to cover the four hundred miles from Creel to Dell City in five days, an average speed of eight miles per hour, twelve hours a day, off-road through the unforgiving high desert. Mawiya insists on taking the two Sisterhood captives with them, considering it a form of rehabilitation that will break them down and win their loyalty. There are two paths to deprogramming violent extremists: torture, which rarely works, and empathy, which takes time but often yields permanent results. The latter comes naturally to the peaceful Raramuri, and torture would be anathema to *Korima*, their creed of unconditional sharing and love. It's a tried-and-true method for therapists, counter-radicalism experts, and skilled hostage-takers—the Stockholm Syndrome, a process that enables loyalty to the captor. Mawiya doesn't know about Stockholm Syndrome, but he has a notion that the two women could be trump cards when push comes to shove in any confrontation with the Sisterhood. And since he is dealing, they can be willing players at his table after a four-hundred-mile run during the dead of summer over the mountains, across the desert sand, and through the canyons of northern Mexico and Far West Texas.

Caba tosses two pairs of thin-soled huaraches to the Sisters, who have not been bound in any way since the first few days of their captivity and who are largely free to roam around the village. The risk of flight is minimal under the watchful eyes of the community, and barefoot, they wouldn't go far enough or fast enough to escape. The Sisters, oblivious to the preparations around them for the journey, are finishing a stew of beans and corn when Caba drops the shoes next to them, then sets a jug of *pinole* on the table.

"The fuck?" questions one of the Sisters.

"Good morning, ladies," Caba says. "You'll need these."

"And?" the other Sister asks.

"Wrong question," says Mawiya, who walks out of the hut and hands each of them a knapsack. "Shoes for running, *pinole* for energy. A few other things in the bag. Nothing surprising: Band-Aids, water, salt, hats. Please put them on."

"Where are we going?" asks the first Sister.

"Texas," says Mawiya.

"The fuck you say?"

"*Cuales son tus nombres?*" asks Caba.

"Succubus," says one Sister, a name Mother gave to her that refers to a female demon who seduces men in their sleep and kills them during sex.

"Uh-huh. And you?" says Caba, gesturing to the other one.

"Hecate," she answers.

"Greek mythology?" says Mawiya. "Good and evil. We'll find the good."

"Cut the crap," says Caba, bad cop to Mawiya's good cop.

"Betty," Succubus answers.

"Anemone," answers the other. "Means *wind*. I was called Annie, before the shit."

"*Muy bien*," Mawiya says. "Betty and Annie it is. Gear up. We're going for a run."

The Copper Canyon, Barranca del Cobre, home of the Raramuri, is a vast network of peaks as high as 8,000 feet and valleys as low as 1,800 in the Sierra Madre Occidental Mountains. Named for the copper-green hue of the canyon walls, it's no walk in the park for the most experienced hiker and, at pace, nothing short of torture for the Sisters. To make matters worse, they are following the path of the famous Chepe train, a popular tourist attraction before the Fall with eighty dark tunnels and forty vertiginous bridges. By the time they reach the Recohuata Hot Springs in San Juanito, twenty miles and a full day's run north from Creel, Betty and Annie are a hot mess of twisted ankles and skinned knees, so dehydrated, hungry, and demoralized that they don't know whether to beg for mercy or pray for death. Only twenty miles and one day from Creel, they are already a lifetime from the Sisterhood and their noms de guerre, Succubus and Hecate. Stumbling toward the turquoise waters of the pools at the spring-fed hot springs of the Recohuata, they are simply Betty and Annie, two former psychology majors at the University of Texas who want nothing more than a long soak, a good meal, a massage, and sleep. Mawiya is happy to oblige.

"We're done for the day," says Mawiya, stripping down and diving into the warm water. With no hesitation, Betty and Annie peel off their sweat-soaked clothes and are in the water within seconds, where they stay for more than an hour nursing their aching muscles and wounded spirits.

Mawiya props himself against a Mexican white pine and peels ripe tangerines they brought from Creel, popping the slices into his mouth as fast as he can strip the rind. Peel, pop. Peel, pop. The sweet, sticky nectar sprays from the fruit every time he slides his thumb under the skin. He plays the slices on his teeth for a moment, titillating the fruit like a woman's erect nipple, until a few drops of juice slide over his tongue. Mawiya is a greedy lover. Cool moisture slides down his throat when he bites down hard. A few drops trickle over his chin. Those that don't fall on his shirt are an aphrodisiac for ants who seem to have been waiting just out of sight for a sweetness they've never known. Mawiya brushes the vanguard of the colony off his pants, palms four tangerines, and walks to the Sisters, who huddle close enough to the fire for warmth but far enough away to express their distaste for captivity. It is a hollow gesture of defiance and a vestige of contempt that has begun to peel from them like the skin of a tangerine from its fruit. Mawiya senses this as he squats next to the two women, who have been transfixed by the Raramuri chieftain's foreplay with the tangerine. Their mouths are not the only part of their bodies that are wet, long-forgotten responses they have not felt since the caress of a man before the Fall. Mawiya peels all four tangerines, close enough to Betty and Annie that they can smell the sweet citrus tang, and holds the fruit to them in his open palm.

"Take," he says, which they do like shy lovers undressing before a man for the first time. They accept the tangerines tentatively, but the rush of passion for the sweet, juicy, cool fruit overwhelms everything, and they take the flesh into their bodies. Sweet surrender. As soon as the crescendo of pleasure passes, they ask for more, and Mawiya, the greedy lover, gives it to them. The intimate exchange repeats itself several times over the next hour until the partners in this ménage à trois are sated. Mawiya moves closer, touching Annie's foot gently as a way of asking how it feels. She understands without words.

"Sore," she responds.

Mawiya begins slowly, as if he is coaxing the fruit of a tangerine from its skin, pushing harder on every knot he finds in her arch. Annie moans, sliding forward toward him with the other foot, a gesture in another type of circumstance that would signal eager capitulation. Betty flinches when Mawiya takes her foot in his hand, but eases into the feeling as his fingers dance over her feet, her ankles, and her calves. The two women are almost asleep afterward when Mawiya stops.

"Let's talk," he says, and they snap back to reality.

"Thank you," Annie says.

"Ditto," Betty seconds.

"*Eschuchame*," Mawiya says.

"We're listening," Annie responds.

"*Presta atencion*."

"We are."

"We are sinners," he says. "All of us. Necessity is not absolution. *Comprende?*"

"Confession," Betty says, "or what?"

"*No es necesaria*," he replies. "I'm no priest."

"What are you?" Annie asks.

"A human," he replies. "Like you. Frail before the power of the universe. But part of it, just a small part. You too, both of you. I am connected to you. We are connected to it all. The dirt, the trees, the water, tangerines, everything. If I can forgive you, it all forgives you. But you must forgive yourself first. Give that to yourselves."

Mawiya is a man of few words. But those few he shares with Betty and Annie have a powerful, subtle effect on them. They say nothing in response. Memories of the obscenities they have witnessed and instigated under Mother flash in their minds: the bull ring, the lynchings, the mating rituals, the slaughters. It is as if the past is like a receding tide and the present is like the beach left exposed when the water retreats to reveal all that has been floating between continents since the beginning of time—the treasures that have always been just below the surface suddenly revealed. And they are transformed into children with small plastic buckets skipping from one delight to the other, collecting keepsakes to set on a shelf as reminders of the beauty and intentional serendipity of life. This good, warm feeling follows them to sleep. But the tide always turns. And Betty realizes it just before she nods off. *Forgiveness comes at a price*, she thinks to herself. Night may have cashed a check that morning can't cover.

Annie—straightforward, forthright, and at her core the trusting daughter of an Evangelical preacher who rose to some prominence from the pulpit of a megachurch in Waco—is not a hard case like Betty. She bought into Mother's brainwashing as easily as she followed her father's heavy-handed fire and brimstone. A clever little chameleon. But Betty, raised in the lap of luxury, is a different story altogether. Her father was a successful independent oilman in Houston, taking over West Texas oil leases that were still producing but not at a volume that interested the bigs, and making his fortune from the bottom of the barrel, so to speak. She was a nerd by Texas standards, bookish due to her mother, but a physically imposing girl and a formidable force as a goalie on the lacrosse team at the uber-elite St. John's High School. Betty was a feminist, at least a Texas prep-school version of one, who brandished her unshaven armpits and legs like a flag of protest and teen sensuality. Because she could, Betty seduced her English lit professor and carried on an illicit romance until he refused to divorce, after which a teary-eyed Betty claimed abuse, and the hapless teacher was sacked. Betty understood power and learned at an early age how to gain what she wanted by manipulating powerful people. After the Fall, all she wanted was to stay alive, a natural fit for the Sisterhood and a favorite of Mother. Of course, Betty knew it was all wrong but could live with it as long as she was still breathing. Deep down, she didn't see herself as a bad person and was willing to go along with the obscenity of life after the Fall until an opening came that would lead her out of it.

But Mawiya and the Raramuri are different, authentic in a way that she's coveted throughout her entire phony life. After only a few days with them, Betty understands for the first time that authenticity, like forgiveness, will come at a price. As she nods off after that first day on the trail, Betty decides that she will bear the cost, even if the price tag is her life.

Betty and Annie begin to emerge as women-in-full over the next three days. The miles and the days of running stretch behind them as the Texas border nears. Their bodies harden as their spirits open to the core belief of the Raramuri, the *Korima*. Mawiya coaxes, teases radicalism out of them in every small gesture: a hand up, a Band-Aid, or a jug of *tesgüino* by the fire. Where hatred resided, *Korima* takes root. The truest test of the Sisters could come in the days ahead as they enter West Texas, America, where *Korima* is in short supply as the showdown between Mother and Ademar nears.

"*Peligro*," Mawiya cautions his people the evening before they enter the Pegüis Canyon and cross the mountain pass into Ojinaga on the Texas border. They all know why it could be dangerous, none more than Betty and Annie, who have ridden with their Sisters on raiding parties on both sides of the frontier between Texas and Mexico. All the Raramuri unsheathe their weapons: rifles, handguns, compound bows, knives, spears, and slingshots. Caba looks at the two women, his eyes cutting to Mawiya as if to ask, *What about them?*

"No, *gracias*," Annie says. Betty shifts nervously from foot to foot, not nearly as confident as Annie in her transformation or as certain she can resist the allure of Mother. Betty imagines what a hero she would be, how she would be elevated to the Sisterhood Council by bringing in the Raramuri as prized captives. An important piece removed from the board in the deadly chess game against the Free People of West Texas.

A network of tributaries from the Rio Conchos River flows through the Pegüis, ten miles of soaring vertical walls and deep slot canyons named after the divine white winged horse in Greek mythology, and join the Rio Grande along the border. A weir had been constructed on the other side of the canyon to divert water into a network of irrigation canals for farmers around Ojinaga. The system is dangerous and unpredictable during the monsoons of August, and nobody needs to be reminded that this is August.

The Raramuri have been watching a line of thunderheads moving toward them as they descend from the pass through a dry slot canyon. A single bolt of lightning cracks the sky and strikes the ground behind them like a coiled rattlesnake. A stand of mesquite trees bursts into flame, and rain pours from the sky. Mawiya, who has experienced a flash flood in a slot canyon, picks up the pace as a trickle of water begins to form pools around them. Within minutes they are sprinting through rushing water up to their waists that spews out of the canyon mouth like a torn fire hose a few hundred yards ahead and just above the weir. They make it, barely, Caba grabbing Betty at the last moment as she tumbles past him.

"Close call," Mawiya says.

"Not as close as that," says Caba, pointing to ten Sisters on the other side of the weir.

The crack of a rifle echoes off the canyon walls, and a rock splinters just above their heads. Water and fire behind them, Sisters ahead, there's no pathway for escape. They slide down a narrow, muddy trail to a rock outcrop that offers shelter near the raging torrent cresting over the weir. Bullets ricochet around the Raramuri, and a rock shard blinds Betty's left eye. The only escape, desperate and dangerous, is the water. But they will need covering fire trained on the Sisters more than three hundred yards away, out of range for Mawiya's .30-30.

"Give me your gun," Betty says to him. "I'll scoot down and hold them off until you're out of range."

"Betty, no!" Annie yells over the rushing water and the cascade of bullets pelting the rock around them. "There's got to be another way."

"There's not," Betty says.

"She's right," says Mawiya, handing the rifle stock-first and a box of shells to Betty, blood running down her cheek from the shriveled left eye socket. "How can you aim with that eye?"

"I aim with my right," Betty says with a sassy, crooked grin Annie hasn't seen since their days at UT.

She begins to scoot down the mud to within range of the Sisters but stops and turns back to Betty, Mawiya, and the rest of them. "Forgiveness comes at a price," she says and is gone.

"What now?" Caba asks.

"Wait for it," Mawiya answers. "When it starts, run like hell for the water."

"I can't swim," Annie says.

"Stay close to me," Mawiya says.

They don't have to wait long, and it is something to behold. Shrouded in ground lightning like an avenging demon, rain pouring around her, Betty stands up just across the water no more than fifty yards from the Sisters. She is fast but methodical, firing and levering another round into the chamber. Two Sisters fall to the ground as Betty walks toward them with the rifle at her shoulder. Fearless. Unprotected. A sitting duck. Fire, reload. Fire, reload. Another Sister falls to the ground.

"Now!" Mawiya yells, and they all sprint toward the water.

They are bobbing in the raging torrent within seconds, except for Annie, who is standing by the water's edge shaking like a leaf, and Mawiya, who takes her hand.

"Trust me," he says, and they leap into the water.

Annie is immediately dragged under by a strong hydraulic, but Mawiya does not let go as the two of them are held down for almost a minute. Mawiya knows from experience that the current will spit them out, and kicks hard for the vortex at the bottom of the hydraulic despite Annie's frantic struggle against him. The spinning aquatic tornado finally grabs them. Their heads pop up above the water, Annie gasping for breath, Mawiya wrapping an arm around her and guiding the two of them downstream. Before they round a bend out of eyesight of the skirmish, they look back toward Betty, firing, reloading, holding the line against the Sisters. Betty jerks twice, falls backward hard. She rises again, firing, reloading. Her head snaps to the side, and she falls for the final time.

"Forgiven," Mawiya whispers into Annie's ear, and they are around the bend.

CHAPTER 19

AFTER THE FALL

The tower guard at the Free People's compound in Dell City at first mistakes the whirlwind for a dust devil, a strong, well-formed miniature tornado common in West Texas. Harmless, unless it hurls a tumbleweed or prickly-pear pad your way. It reminds him of *The Wizard of Oz* and such banal indulgences before the Fall as evenings nodding off in front of the television with an empty Lone Star in his lap, kids asleep, and nothing more to worry about than another day at the office. Perimeter guard duty at the compound is a deadly serious business, particularly on the eve of war with a duplicitous enemy like the Sisterhood, and he keeps the high-powered binoculars trained on the swirling dust in the distance. A band of horsemen shrouded in dust emerges from the haze, and the guard sounds the alarm.

"Riders!"

The compound, only a few seconds earlier a pastoral mural in the mold of Grant Wood's *American Gothic*, explodes to life like a beehive swatted by a hungry grizzly. Dozens of men and women grab weapons, chamber rounds, and rush to the positions they have been trained to take in drill after drill. A self-propelled 155 mm howitzer backs out of a barn with T3 at the wheel, and Ademar, wiggling into her flak jacket, strides out of the front door of the main house. She is the maestro of this well-oiled orchestra of destruction, and, as for any conductor, all eyes turn to her for the opening stroke of a baton.

"Steady," she says, not quite a yell but hardly conversational. Like a woman half her age, Ademar, skipping every other rung on the steel ladder, ascends to the nest at the top of the guard tower. The sentinel hands her the binoculars, and, for a few seconds, those few seconds before every battle when every soldier thinks the long hours of waiting are over, silence settles over the compound. Ademar smiles and lowers the binoculars when three riders emerge from the dust. White Eagle, stripped to the waist and waving his battle lance as if he is greeting an old friend, which he is, trots slightly in front of two others at the head of the pack. Stone and Charlie Christmas flank him, with the other twenty-two riders not far behind.

Ademar cups her hands around her mouth. "Stand down. Friendlies."

They are a formidable force, the kind of Sioux raiding party that in another era struck fear into the hearts of homesteaders from West Texas to the Dakotas. Back then, a mere whisper of such a war party had frantic sodbusters ushering women and children into basements, pulling rifles off walls, and securing every entrance to the house with wooden shutters secured by planks and steel braces. But they are friendlies, old ones, and family.

"Sight for sore eyes," Stone says to Ademar, who helps the old warrior down from his horse. "I'm obliged."

"Not the youngest anymore, Cap."

"You're telling me."

"White Eagle, Charlie, welcome," Ademar says. "How was it?"

"Rough," Charlie says. "Run-in with the Sisters, two biker dudes with them, on horses. Dead. Five down."

"Clouds are forming," White Eagle says. "The storm is upon us. Word of our Arwen?"

"Yes," Ademar says. "A note, and demands from Mother."

"Good," White Eagle says. "She's alive."

"Make yourselves at home," says Ademar, gesturing to the sprawling compound. "Get cleaned up. We'll talk it out over dinner. Ride tomorrow to Rancho Seco."

Rancho Seco has been like Valhalla for generations of the Laws and Zarkan families. When they sold it decades ago to a prosperous El Paso family, it was several hundred acres of undeveloped West Texas scrub hard against the Guadalupe Mountains outside Dell City. Jack Laws charged his old friends from El Paso only a few dollars an acre, under the condition that he would have keys to the gates and hunting rights in perpetuity. Succeeding generations developed the property into a rustic, no-frills retreat for friends and family: latrines, not toilets, and screened cabins with pot-bellied stoves. Over the years, due mostly to two sons with a knack for engineering and construction, they installed solar, built a propane-heated shower nook, and cultivated a drip-irrigated pistachio grove, all controlled from afar with iPhone apps. So many of the small events and rites of passage transpired there: Crockett Laws, Deuce's father, shot his first deer under Jack's watchful eye; Ademar and Deuce made love for the first time after their high school prom; and the families spread the ashes of T2 and Anil after the terrorist incident in Brussels, to name a few. The ethos of Rancho Seco, the true expression of the families and of the high desert, was the circular maze a matriarch of the El Paso family built near the foothills of the Guadalupes. Originally just a secluded, slightly spooky corner of Rancho Seco for her to play with grandchildren or tell ghost stories around a fire, it grew over the years into sacred ground, Stonehenge on the high desert for generations of the El Paso family. And there, in the heart of the circular maze, is where Ademar plans to convene her war council in preparation for an engagement with the Sisterhood that will preserve or destroy their way of life.

Despite the absence of a critical piece in the alliance, Mawiya and the Raramuri, the rest of them set out on horseback for Rancho Seco. They gather at the old high school near the defunct Two T's grocery, a shell with faded candy wrappers and rusted cans of spam strewn amid the tumbleweeds. The faded glory of America reduced to its worst common denominator. Star, her broken leg fully healed, sniffs among the trash for something interesting or edible. A few hundred years ago they could have been a platoon of US Cavalry riding after Comanches holed up in the Guadalupe Mountains that tower over Dell City in the east, or, more recently, dust bowl migrants trekking across the high desert toward greener pastures in California. No doubt some of the bleached bones out there are the lonely remnants of past battles and lost dreams.

Ademar and her crew are not dreamers. They are realists, hardened veterans of the Fall who have no intention of leaving their bones for the carrion birds that patrol the sky for the corpses of the vanquished. They're not in a hurry on the paved road east out of town toward 1576 that connects to Van Horn and the dilapidated El Capitan hotel and saloon, an Old West encyclopedia of gunfights and card games. Lines of pivot sprinklers, like steel spiderwebs, span the green fields and spew water over cantaloupes, onions, chili peppers, and tomatoes, a testament to the resiliency of the Free People of West Texas and to the solar-powered pumps that suck water from the Bone Spring–Victorio Peak Aquifer. Ademar, Stone, Charlie, and White Eagle leave the paved road heading dead east across the Salt Flats and will find themselves amid a different set of skeletons, the rusted steel of Jeff Bezos's Blue Origin rocket launch site, if they don't cut back north toward Rancho Seco after a few miles. Legend has it that Bezos, his family, and a handful of "important" people launched themselves into space before the Fall more than two years ago. Interstellar migrants now most likely corpses rotting in cryogenic chambers that have run out of the liquid nitrogen meant to preserve them in suspended animation three hundred degrees below zero until the castaways drift ashore on another planet.

"Think they're still up there?" Noah asks Amiir.

"Something's up there," says Stone, pointing to a bleached longhorn skull in the dirt. "Wager they look like that if they still are."

"Death and taxes," Ademar says. "They avoided taxes. The other, doubt it."

The pistachio grove between the pavilion and the hunter's cabin at Rancho Seco seemed untouched by the Fall, due mainly to the solar-powered drip irrigation system that still provided two hundred gallons of water weekly from the aquifer to the trees. Noah and Amiir gather pistachios while Stone stokes the coals under the grate of a barbecue grill a member of the El Paso family designed and a metalsmith forged out of molten steel. Ingenious and simple, really, like all things that endure: a three-inch steel pole standing two feet out of cement with a grate attached by an arm that encircled the pole and pivoted over the fire. Like many of the improvements, this one was installed with the help of a friend from the East who grew up in Texas and made the pilgrimage to West Texas every now and then to stay in touch with his roots. A journalist and writer, a fish out of water in the East, he and his kids survived the Fall with a harrowing journey back home to command the Free People's redoubt in what was once Sul Ross State University. Stone pulls the steaks off the grill and the Idahos wrapped in aluminum foil from the coals. He plucks the garlic heads off the grate and squeezes the viscous meat over the steaks until it pools with butter oozing out of the steaming potatoes. Throw in an iced longneck apiece for each of them, and for a few moments, just a few, they can forget the Fall and the stakes of the task before them.

"Wrap it up," Ademar says after the feast. "Stone, Charlie, White Eagle, Deuce—the maze."

Star, ever vigilant, paces the perimeter while the five of them squat on stones encircling a pile of totems deposited over the years atop the ashes of the dead: Jack, Marcie, T2, Anil, more than a few loyal canines, and dirt from three continents where Stone led soldiers into battle. There is Charlie's necklace with the tiny carved white ptarmigan, the letter *S*, the 7.62 mm shell, the eagle-bone whistle, the Somali flag and the Islamic crescent, and the king from the chess set a friend of Charlie's son carved in prison. The fire and glowing sparks in rusting fifty-gallon drums around the maze reaches toward the sky and dances around them in the wind like tiny glowing stars. White Eagle sits cross-legged at the burning-barrel summit, puffing on a pipe and passing it around.

Ademar reads aloud Arwen's letter: "*Dear Abuela, if there are any children left in this world, I am not one of them . . .*"

Ademar and Deuce are as indignant now as the first time they read it around the pecan table in the great room at their compound. Fury and revenge are the zeitgeist of the moment. Stone feels it, as he felt it after a Somali warlord kidnapped an American helicopter pilot during the botched raid on Bakaara Market in central Mogadishu. He knows that success hinges on cool heads and does the best imitation of himself as a forty-year-old Army captain.

"Okay," Stone says. "Chill."

"Sir," says Ademar, smiling at the return of the Captain Stone she first met in Somalia four decades ago.

"Lieutenant," says Stone, hearkening back to those days when Lieutenant Zarkan was a green West Point graduate assigned to Stone's unit. "A lot of water under the bridge, Ademar."

"True that," says Charlie, who was Ademar's translator in Somalia.

"Objective?" asks Stone, running through the components of a battle plan.

"Ademar," Deuce replies.

"Strategy?"

"Walk softly, carry a big stick," Ademar says. "Negotiate if we can. Fight if we must."

"Tactics?"

"The Raramuri," White Eagle whispers.

"What do you mean?" Ademar says. "They're dead, God forbid, for all we know. Have to fight with the army we have."

"They are alive," White Eagle says. "I know it. Like the white buffalo, they will appear. So will the whale."

"*Inshallah*," says Charlie.

"Simple," says Stone. "Hail Mary. Hope for the best, prepare for the worst. Our secret weapon, and they may not even be alive. Recipe for disaster."

"I know, Cap," Ademar says.

"Fuck me," Stone says. "No choice."

"Faith," White Eagle says. "That's what we have."

CHAPTER 20

AFTER THE FALL

From the beginning, there was no daylight between Deuce, Ademar, and her older brother, T2. Equal in almost all ways: hunting, farming, riding, studying, and navigating life in the small high desert town of Dell City, population five hundred. Of course, Ademar was a girl, but that didn't hardly register until they were well into their teens. Ademar was the quintessential tomboy, so much so that her mother wondered if she might favor girls over boys, especially after she kissed a competitor on the lips in the barn after the women's high school barrel-racing championship. Lithe, muscular, and tough as a boot, Ademar knew she was a match for any boy and proved it by winning a spot as kicker on the high school six-man football team. The first inkling Deuce had that his feelings for Ademar might be more than friendship came during football tryouts, when Coach K insisted she jump in on an Oklahoma, a one-on-one tackling drill that separates the men from the boys, and the girls. She outsmarted the ball carrier at the line with a shoulder dip and made a tackle worthy of her older brother, who would go on to play D1 linebacker at the University of

Texas El Paso. Only seventeen and a rank amateur in the ways of romance, Deuce felt a twinge of something different for her that hot August day on the dusty gridiron.

Ademar blossomed into an exotic beauty in her teens, wavy jet-black hair from her Syrian heritage and eyes the deep blue-green of polished turquoise. All her life, Ademar rarely wore anything more than jeans, work boots, a faded denim yoke shirt, and a straw cowboy hat. On more than one occasion, she was mistaken for a boy, which was exactly how she wanted it. No quarter asked; none given. But it was not lost on Deuce when she began to fill out her clothes in ways that brought back that twinge he had during the football drill. Ademar was smart as a whip, scoring nearly perfect scores on her SATs and following Deuce to West Point. But it was a few years prior that the two of them realized they would spend their lives together. Ademar made the first move, holding Deuce gently in her arms and comforting him after he saved her twin brother Anil during a farming accident that took his left hand. She also led Deuce into the ultimate act of intimacy after their high school prom, under a blanket in the back of a pickup at Rancho Seco. The first time for both of them, and a moment of absolute magic beneath the splendor of a full West Texas sky. That singular expression of their love had none of the first-time teen awkwardness or shy fumbling with bra straps and belts. Ademar, mature beyond her years and a natural woman even at seventeen, simply shrugged her dress off, cozied up to Deuce under the blanket, and took him inside of her. Their love endured, and so did their passion, through West Point, wars on two continents, children, and four decades of marriage. And now, especially now, after the Fall.

Lost in their thoughts, unsure of their futures, two years into the apocalypse, and hanging by a thread, the leaders of the burning-barrel summit at the maze shuffle into the night. Ademar takes Deuce's hand in hers and leads him to the four-hundred-gallon stock tank that is always full of cool water, courtesy of the ingenious solar-powered pump that senses the depth and refills it when the level dips a few inches below the rim. She peels off all her clothes, pausing for a seductive moment so Deuce can take in her silhouette against a full moon. A fine silhouette, he thinks, even into her seventies, and he feels that twinge. A lifetime of ranching has held off the ravages of time, so obvious to Deuce now, as she hops into the water. Tight thighs. Full breasts. Firm stomach. And arms without the usual draping skin of a septuagenarian. She is her gift to him, only him, as he is to her. Neither of them are playful types, which makes the playfulness in their lovemaking that much more playful, and private. Ademar presses her palms together, suctions water into them, and squirts it at Deuce. His muscles, the muscles of a former college quarterback, military officer, and West Texas rancher, tense up, and the parts of Ademar's body that have always welcomed him start to welcome him again.

"How about a ride, cowboy?" she says.

"Yes, ma'am," replies Deuce, climbing into the tank, which is barely large enough for both of them.

This is the time when Ademar, the tomboy, yields. Deuce slides his legs around Ademar, takes her ankles into his hands, and pulls both legs around him. She feels him in the most intimate places and shifts her hips forward to open that warm part of her he has known so well. They are in no hurry, skin to skin, savoring every taste, every smell, every small corner of their bodies that only they know. Ademar's tongue traces the jagged scar along his chest, the old knife wound from an ISIS captor, and pinches his nipple with her front teeth. A touch of pain to accompany the pleasure. Deuce moans and returns the favor, pushing himself all the way inside of her. Water sloshes over the side of the tank, and goosebumps rise on their exposed wet skin in the chilly night air of the

desert. They rise from the cool water to re
cowboy bedroll unfurled a few feet away. He t
the rough waterproof canvas, and they slide, laugh
warm fleece lining. Ademar is on him in a second, bc
pulling him into her. They rock back and forth, eyes lo
smiling, for this moment the only two humans in the worl.

When it is over, and it's not over soon, Ademar reaches
into her jeans for the miniature short-wave monitor. For a
few hours every night, the hacker group Anonymous hosts a
music broadcast, and when she turns it on, they are playing
Alan Jackson's "Remember When." It takes them back to their
high school prom.

"I held you this close," says Deuce, pushing the small of
her back so that their chests touch, and the friction arouses
them both.

"I remember," Ademar whispers into his ear, just as she
had on that night so many decades ago that began with a song,
that song, and ended under a blanket just a few hundred yards
from where they are now.

They surrender to each other again. Slow dancing in
the dark.

They move easily from passion to love. Ademar wraps an
arm around Deuce and cradles his head under her arm. Deuce
is not a greedy lover, but he is greedy for this smell, always.
The night is especially dark, the stars spectacularly bright.
And they both know the stakes at hand in the coming battle
with the Sisterhood.

"What if we never have this again?" Deuce asks.

"This will be my last sweet thought as I die," Ademar replies.

A shadow passes over them, a snowy owl silhouetted by
the moon. A few hundred yards away on the steps of the hunters' cabin, White Eagle sees the owl too. For his people, it is
a harbinger of death.

Mother hisses. "Try again."

"...1 me," Arwen says.

"...nk you know," says Mother, holding out the crotch-...ack lace 1950s-era corset. "Now, let's put this on."

"What's that?"

"An outfit for you, princess. Wash yourself and I'll show you."

Arwen emerges from the shower with a towel wrapped tightly around her, and Mother beckons. "Drop the towel," she commands.

"No."

Mother, neck veins bulging in fury, grabs both sides of the towel as if she's jacking up a drunk by the lapels in a bar fight. Arwen sees the sweet spot—Mother's jugular—raises the fingernail file she found in the bathroom, and thrusts down hard. She can almost feel the arterial spray of warm blood. But Mother is quicker, grabbing Arwen's wrist and twisting it until she drops the file.

"Not today, princess," Mother says and rips the towel off the young girl.

Arwen stands naked and vulnerable in front of Mother, who forces her into the corset one foot at a time and pulls it under her arms. Mother spins her around by the hips, yanking the strings that bind the corset until Arwen's breasts poke out like small ripe oranges and she can hardly breathe.

Mother spins her back around. "Lovely." A small patch of bright red hair pokes out of the opening in the crotchless corset. "This has to go. Don't move," says Mother, and in seven strokes of the straight-edge razor, Arwen is shorn. "The finishing touch," says Mother, filling her palm with Astroglide lubricant. She rubs it all over Arwen's freshly shaved parts and, roughly with two fingers, jams it inside of her. Arwen feels something deep in her tear. Mother holds up her blood-smeared fingers. "That will make it easier for you, princess.

"Why is today different from all others?" asks
"I think you know."

The spectacle waiting for them outside is both grand
farcical. *Gladiator* meets *Austin Powers*, with a dash of *Wond*
Woman thrown in for good measure. Arwen suppresses a
laugh. "Pitiful," she says under her breath.

Mother whispers, "You won't think it's so funny in a
few minutes."

The crowd of Sisters, in two lines stretching hundreds of
yards, ululates when Mother holds aloft a tiara forged into the
shape of their symbol, the one tattooed on the shaved side of
their leader's head, a praying mantis devouring its mate during
copulation. A screen of silence rolls across the Sisters when
Mother pulls back Arwen's long, fiery red hair and places the
tiara on her head. The ghoulish ululation rises back up like a
dirge from the inferno. Four men, dragging the kind of two-
wheeled garden cart someone's dad might use to haul potted
plants around the backyard, gallop through the line of Sisters
and stop at the bottom of the stairway leading to Arwen. The
men, Sisterhood captives, are dressed in comical facsimiles of
Roman togas, and the plastic cart has been retrofitted with
a stanchion to resemble the podium on a chariot. Mother,
flanked by two enormous Sisters with spears, nudges Arwen
down the stairs, then onto the cart. She pulls a bullwhip from
a sheath on the cart, waves it in circles over her head like a
cowboy about to toss his lasso at an errant steer, and cracks it
hard enough to draw lines of blood on the backs of the two
men at the front of the cart. They snap to life like whipped
dogs, nearly toppling Arwen and Mother from the cart as they
bolt through the line of Sisters. Mother adjusts Arwen's tiara,
which has fallen cockeyed to one side of her head. She whips
the men mercilessly, maniacally, like a diabolic dervish, one
side and then the other, until they reach the arena where Arwen
witnessed the human bullfight weeks earlier. The spectators,

hundred Sisters, fall silent when the cart comes to rest a wooden dais on which a fully erect man is tied.

"Down," Mother commands Arwen.

"Sisters!" Mother shouts to spectators assembled in the arena. "A few months ago, we plucked this desert flower from our enemies. Arwen Laws, granddaughter of Ademar Zarkan, leader of the Free People of West Texas. Weak. Distracted. Child's play to grab her from their doorstep. Today, we plant another seed for our revolution. The first of many this girl will bear for us. We will slay her sons with their first breath. Her daughters will be our princesses and queens. We are unstoppable. Long live the Sisterhood!"

Mother pauses. Her right eye twitches as a distant memory invades her glorious moment. She is suddenly a teenager pushed in the dirt behind a barn with three strangers raping her over and over. The seconds stretch to minutes. Only Arwen sees the twitching, and senses the past trauma. The moment of shame washes over Mother, and anger, the red anger of a violent, radicalized extremist, takes over. Gone is that Native American victim of drunken, cursing, sweat-stained white men laughing at *Pocahontas* under them. She is no longer Pocahontas. She is Mother: powerful, calculating, cruel, and the mistress of the universe.

Mother commands two Sisters to place Arwen over the man tied to the dais. She is eager to savor the frantic pleas of Ademar Zarkan's beloved granddaughter. But Arwen doesn't struggle, doesn't cry for mercy.

"That's not necessary," says Arwen, smiling, willingly ascending the dais and standing over the man. "I've been looking forward to this."

Arwen has a plan. The nail file was a diversion, an appetizer to whet Mother's appetite for this moment. Now is the time to execute it. She stands over the man, who will penetrate her if she simply sits. But she doesn't.

"Do it!" Mother shouts, and the crowd takes up her command.

"Do it! Do it!"

Brave, proud, unyielding, the thirteen-year-old girl stands ramrod straight, ready to die before her life has hardly begun. She looks Mother straight in the eyes.

"No."

"What did you say, child?"

"You heard me. No."

"Force her!" Mother screams.

"You will never see the whale if you do," Arwen replies. "What you want most will never be yours."

"Wait," says Mother, holding up her hand to the two Sisters on either side of Arwen. "You defy me?" Mother asks Arwen.

"Yes," she replies.

"Are you prepared to die?"

"Yes. Are you prepared to fail?"

"Fail?"

"I have the power to bring the whale to you, and all the power inside of it that you want. You know it. Go ahead, I double dog dare you. Kill me. What will your people think when they realize all your big talk about ruling the world is a bunch of lies? Think about it. You might be the next one they strap the horns on."

Mother's shoulders don't droop; weakness and vulnerability do not a cult leader make. But she is withering inside at the obvious insult and defeat at the hands of a defiant teenager. "You win this round, Arwen," Mother whispers to her. "But I will have that whale."

"At least you won't not have it," Arwen answers.

Mother stares in the frantic, frightened eyes of the man. "Kill him!" she shouts, and a guard drives a spear into his heart. "He is unworthy."

CHAPTER 22

AFTER THE FALL

A journey of a thousand miles begins with a single step, on horseback from South Dakota or on huaraches from Creel. But for 52 Blue, the first step was not a step at all. It was the powerful thrust of a tail propelling four hundred thousand pounds from the frigid Arctic Sea to the tepid Gulf of Mexico. Her journey, no less fraught than the road to Texas for the Raramuri or the Origin Tribes of the Mountain West, will cover six thousand miles, six times longer than that of Mawiya, White Eagle, Stone, and Charlie Christmas. And the blue whale will be alone, as she has been for decades, transmitting clicks and whistles at fifty-two hertz in search of her mate. The sentient mammal hopes she will find her partner on this journey, but that's not what drives 52 Blue to uncharted waters just off the Texas coast. Transporting a nest of hard drives under her back fin, she is the essential piece on the board in a multidimensional chess game that will determine the future of earth and all its inhabitants. 52 Blue—with a twenty-pound brain, seven times heavier than the average human's, and almost supernatural navigation skills that rely on magnetic fields and undersea topography—has no idea what awaits her in Texas. All she has is the connection to the Terra-Algorithm, the collective unconscious of all things, and to a young redheaded girl who communicates in dreams.

52 Blue had a female calf once, a perfect, frolicking companion and expression of love for her mate. She was helpless to stop a great white from tearing her baby apart several years ago on an annual migration near Block Island. Her four-hundred-pound heart broke, and, whatever the reason, she is determined not to float idly by while another kind of shark tears apart another kind of baby.

52 Blue has a favorite song, nothing like Alan Jackson's heartfelt ballad favored by Ademar and Deuce, but a sonorous staccato of clicks she repeats over and over to herself as the miles pass. Hannah Spencer, the scientist in DC who embedded the hard drives inside the whale, identified the song through an undersea microphone, and it helped her track 52 Blue for years. Hannah often wonders what happened to 52 Blue after the Fall, and she will forever be in the big-hearted whale's debt for saving her daughter, Azul. Hannah has no idea how close she was to 52 Blue when the whale started her journey just off the coast of Svalbard, or about the ensuing battle over the hard drives that lie at the end of it.

Nor does 52 Blue, repeating her favorite song as she enters the slightly warmer waters near Long Island Sound. A pod of dolphins, drawn to the pleasing acoustics, join 52 Blue, who could not be happier for some company. She delights in the antics of several dolphin calves, no more than a few months old, and when they nuzzle up to her, it reminds 52 Blue of the offspring she lost to a ravenous great white several years ago not far from Long Island Sound.

Under the watchful eye of their mother, the pod of baby dolphins ventures to a prime surfing break near Montauk, leaping through the curls in unison with the few surfers, defiantly surfing through the apocalypse, standing on colorful odd-shaped fiberglass objects. A few of the other dolphins in the pod stay with 52 Blue, keeping their new friend company as she feeds on krill, eating the small crustaceans that escape her baleen plates. An aquatic version of a cookout by an open fire in West Texas. The calves swim circles around 52 Blue when they return, chattering and chirping like children, interrupting each other to be the first to communicate the magical encounter with the surfers. 52 Blue takes it all in with delight, scanning her eyes from one calf to the next, blinking as she tries to keep up with their stories.

Almost too late, she spots a shadow emerging from the cloudy steel-gray water of the Atlantic. 52 Blue turns her entire four hundred thousand pounds with one swish of the tail, positioning herself, stem to stern, a full one hundred feet, between the calves and whatever it is moving fast toward them. All she sees out of the corner of her left eye is a wake of bubbles, but she feels the grip of razor-sharp teeth, the rip of flesh, and she knows in an instant it's a shark. 52 Blue's pirouette saved the calves, but, as blood seeps from the gash where there was once a two-pound slab of blubber, the whale knows she's in for a fight with an undersea menace no less deadly than the Sisterhood.

She senses Arwen—tossing, turning in her bed at the Sisterhood compound, dripping wet with sweat as she watches the nightmare unfold in real time—and wants to reassure the girl thousands of miles away that it will be okay. *Just a scratch*, 52 Blue thinks to herself, points her nose toward the surface, flips her tail, and rises almost entirely from the ocean. In midair, she turns, head perpendicular to the surface, bead on the shark below with its jaws wide open. 52 Blue, all four hundred thousand pounds, crashes into the great white at the exact moment two dolphins surge from the depths and bludgeon the underbelly of the predator. The unconscious shark floats like a leaf to the bottom of the sea, seemingly lifeless, but comes to life when it lands on the floor in a poof of sand.

The great white attempts to turn back to the whale and its deputies, to renew the attack, but something is broken deep inside, and it swims away awkwardly, crippled. The mother dolphin gathers her frightened calves while others in the pod inspect 52 Blue's wound, hardly a scratch but by no means life threatening. The whale heads south, and the dolphins, in a phalanx around their friend, accompany her several hundred miles along the Eastern Seaboard. The dolphins stop off the coast of North Carolina, touch noses with 52 Blue, and head back north. The whale is left alone again with her favorite song, and nightly visits from Arwen, with whom she has unfinished business off the coast of Texas.

52 Blue swings west off the coast of Florida, avoiding shark-infested waters, weaving her way through the underwater canyons south of the Rokers Point Settlement in the Bahamas. She circles east, meditating through the long journey by repeating her favorite song, hoping against hope that it might attract her mate. Tracing the coast of Cuba, from Guantanamo Bay to Trinidad, she veers south around the Isla de la Juventud to avoid any trouble with fishermen trolling the waters out of Nueva Gerona. Just south of Cuba, before she turns sharply north into the Gulf of Mexico and heads to Texas, 52 Blue passes over an undersea communications cable.

Named after the Bolivarian Alliance for the Peoples of Our America, Alianza Bolivariana para los Pueblos de Nuestra America, ALBA-1 was a submarine communications cable activated in 2013 by the Venezuelan government to create a link between Caracas and Havana, totalitarian anomalies in the Western Hemisphere allied with Moscow and Beijing. It has lain dormant since the Fall when the hacker group Anonymous flipped off the switch of everything, although 52 Blue sees clearly what an experienced oceanographer would instantly recognize as a remote-camera attachment panning 360 degrees. The whale swims right up to the camera, and a red light on top flashes when she bumps it lightly with her nose.

A small distraction in a long journey, like a stop at a Waffle House on Route 66 for a vacationing American family before the Fall. The whale doesn't even stop singing until she hears a distant set of clicks and hums that could possibly be her mate. Like an aquatic metronome, 52 Blue scans the surrounding waters and, several hundred yards away, spies a cigar-shaped object that looks very much like a whale. Tracing the path of ALBA-1, she swims closer for a better look, and the closer she gets, the more it looks like a whale, except for a tentacle stretching to the cable. The clicks and hums, distinctly mechanical, are foreign sounds to her, clearly not the song of a whale. 52 Blue doesn't realize this until a steel arm shoots from the object and encircles her with a sturdy steel-cable net. A shout of victory comes from inside the boat, and the captain of the North Korean submarine flashes a thumbs-up to his crew. He engages a lever inside the Sinpo-C ballistic missile submarine, their most advanced model before the Fall, and the cable tightens around 52 Blue until she is completely immobile. She tries to thrash, eyes wide and panicked with no hope for rescue, and another arm shoots out from the submarine. A circular saw attached to the end of this arm comes alive when the captain pushes a button on his control panel, and the whirring diamond-steel blade extends toward the whale's head.

The Sisterhood is not the only group chasing the hard drives embedded in 52 Blue. The media reports of their theft were not lost on Russia, China, and their ally North Korea. The Fall crippled the nuclear-powered naval fleets of the great powers, but not the diesel-powered submarines of Pyongyang. And, at the behest of China and Russia, they have roamed the world's oceans in search of her the past two years. They knew

52 Blue's favorite song from the recordings made by Hannah Spencer, which were readily available through open-source technology, and that's how they located her off the coast of Cuba. With diesel fuel dwindling, they had lost hope of finding her and retrieving the hard drives, until today. The North Korean captain could have cared less that he might be driving blue whales into extinction. The glory of tiny North Korea, Moscow and Beijing's slipper boy for decades before the Fall, is all he thinks about as the blade comes within inches of 52 Blue's head.

52 Blue is almost relieved that her life, and her endless lonely quest, is coming to an end. She relaxes into the net and waits for the inevitable: pain, death, then whatever comes after. She has forgotten about Arwen, until the telepathy of the young girl reaches her. She can see Arwen in her bed at the Sisterhood compound, hear her as if she is floating there, and feel the young girl's tender touch across her dorsal fin.

"It's not over," Arwen whispers.

At that exact moment, the blade stops, and the submarine engines fall silent. A digital deity, a faceless human wearing the Guy Fawkes mask of Anonymous, flashes on the monitor in front of the North Korean captain. Anonymous may have destroyed the infrastructure of everything, but they still maintain some digital functionality through the network of undersea cables. And tracking North Korean submarines is one of them. The human in the mask raises a finger, waving it side to side in the universal sign of *no*. The arm of the submarine falls limp, and the steel net around 52 Blue eases enough for her to wriggle free. With four whips of her powerful tail, the whale is heading north into the Gulf of Mexico at thirty miles per hour. When 52 Blue pauses to look back from what feels like a safe distance, all she sees is the North Korean submarine stuck nose-first into the ocean floor.

CHAPTER 23

AFTER THE FALL

This is the moment of truth before the moment of truth. Every battle has one. Those few hours, usually in the pre-dawn darkness, when a commander walks from trench to trench, fire to fire, barracks to barracks, or aircraft to aircraft shaking hands, sharing legends, reassuring recruits and veterans—men and women—reminding them of nothing more in particular than their mission and their honor. Alexander the Great. Charlemagne. Grant. Patton. Stone knows this moment. He's had it in Iraq, Somalia, Bosnia-Herzegovina, Kosovo. Charlie Christmas knows Stone in these moments: before they boarded a Black Hawk for an assault on Bakaara Market in Mogadishu and before they rescued his son Amiir from a Kenyan refugee camp. Stone-cold. Standing next to Stone behind a sand dune on Matagorda Island, the northern tip of Padre along the Texas coast, Charlie knows what comes next. The pace, the rhythm, the customs of Stone, Charlie knows them so well after so many years. Stone squats, scoops up a bit of sand, and pours it from his palm into a small film canister. Before the Fall, certain no more battles lay ahead,

Stone emptied the earthen souvenirs from all his wars on the pile of totems in the middle of the maze at Rancho Seco. Now, he has one more.

"Where's that going, brother?" says Charlie, wrapping an arm around Stone's shoulder.

"Where else?" Stone says. "After. If there's an after."

It's different for Mother, gathered with her Sisters at the edge of the water, a quarter mile away on the other side of the dunes. It's always different for the aggressor, who rarely has the moral high ground to make the case for honor. Theirs is the case for greed and power, backed by fear of a ruthless leader who sees them only as pawns. Mother smells the fear as she walks the lines of Sisters on the beach. She has little to say, merely nodding or holding up a clenched fist as a symbol that neither reassures nor comforts. Mother stops and turns to the two lieutenants accompanying her on the rounds.

"They're nervous, scared," one of them says.

"They will fight," she says. "Or else."

"Thought this was a negotiation," the Sister says.

"Fuck negotiations," Mother says.

Stone hears the banter of Noah and Amiir a few dozen yards away. "1973," says Noah, passing the time with their favorite game.

"Dude, 1973?" says Amiir, answering a question with a question.

"Watergate," Noah says.

"Yeah, Watergate," says Stone, tossing a Snickers on the ground between the two boys, who grab the candy before Star can get to it. "Nixon, the break-in, Woodward, Bernstein."

"Right," says Amiir, pretending to remember it from his history class before the Fall.

"Know what you're doing in the morning?" Stone asks.

"Yes," they say in unison.

"Say it," Stone says.

"Stay back, hold the dunes, no heroics," they say.

"Affirmative," Stone says. "Now get some sleep, knuckle-heads."

Stone walks among the Indigenous warriors applying face paint and handprints on their horses, sharpening spears, checking rifles. During his Army days, he had many Native Americans under his command, like Blacks and Hispanics, often the cannon fodder for an invasion. As a Jew, Stone knows the sharp end of injustice and persecution. He treats every man and woman with even-handedness, humility, and respect, the least he can offer in return for their lives. Stone walks by their fires, calling each warrior by name, shaking hands, cracking jokes.

"No scalps," says Stone, with a wry smile.

"Just yours," quips one of them, smiling.

"Slim pickings," says Stone, passing a palm over what's left of his hair.

Ademar, Deuce, T3, White Eagle, and his wife, Red Thunder, are sitting around a fire discussing strategy when Stone walks up and takes a knee next to them. He pulls five cigars from his jacket pocket.

"Saved these," he says, passing one to each of them, along with a lighter.

"White man's tobacco," says Red Thunder, and they all laugh.

"Cubans," says Stone. "Castro. Brown man."

"Thank you," White Eagle says. "I'll save it for after."

"Tomorrow—here's how I see it," says Stone, sketching the battlefield in the sand with his finger. "Talk first. Deuce and I meet Mother and her banshees halfway. Try to negotiate Arwen's release."

"With what?" Ademar asks. "She's made it crystal clear it's got to be that whale, those hard drives."

"No way," Deuce says. "She gets those, game over."

"Subterfuge," Stone says. "Has to believe she's getting them."

"How?" asks Ademar.

"Not how," answers Stone, pulling out a flask of sotol, taking a pull, and passing it on. "When."

"Go on," White Eagle says.

"Let's be honest," says Stone. "Tomorrow will be a fight, not a negotiation. Best we can hope for is time and space to grab Arwen. Our resident sharpshooter, Ademar, stays back, takes Mother out when the talks fail, which they will."

"How will we know?" asks Ademar. "Two hundred yards away."

"I kick the sand," Stone answers. "Pull the trigger and keep pulling it. Double tap 'em all."

"Then what?" asks Charlie.

"Then all hell breaks loose," Stone replies, turning to White Eagle. "Then bring it. Everyone charges. Straight at the fuckers. Full frontal."

"That's a shitty plan," Ademar says. "You and Deuce are gonna grab Arwen and hold off fifty Sisters until the cavalry arrives? Sitting ducks."

"Got a better idea?" asks Stone.

"Yes," Red Thunder says. "Mawiya, the Raramuri."

"In case you haven't noticed," says Stone, "ain't here."

"Just wait," White Eagle says.

"You know something we don't?" says Ademar.

"Yes," says White Eagle.

CHAPTER 24

AFTER THE FALL

B attles are won or lost on the details. Stone, with twenty years of it under his belt; Ademar and Deuce, who studied it at West Point and executed it on three continents; and T3, a veteran of Iraq and Afghanistan, know it, breathe it, feel it. That's why they chose the dunes above the beach to the east.

"Downhill, sun behind us," says Stone, standing at the crest of the dunes as the first arc of flaxen light ascends the horizon behind him, and morning creeps across the water toward the Sisters in formation along the beach. "Right, Zarkan?"

"The small things, Cap," Ademar replies.

In the annals of warfare, the dimensions of this battle don't hold a candle to history: Thermopylae, Gettysburg, Verdun, Normandy, Khe Sanh, Medina Ridge, Kyiv. But the stakes are higher than all of them together. The next few minutes will determine the future of humankind.

Everyone is in position. *El momento de la verdad.* "Show-time," says Stone as he and Deuce walk down the dunes toward the sea. The wind picks up with each step, and the footprints behind them vanish. Halfway to the water, no prints behind or ahead—castaways in the uncharted future of everything.

Ademar, Charlie Christmas by her side, follows their progress through the high-powered laser scope on her .30-30, probably not the ideal rifle for long-range sniping, but the one she knows best. She scans the shoreline and finds Mother, only the second time she has laid eyes on the Sisterhood leader, with Arwen, alive, next to her. Muscle memory from her sniper days takes over: crosshairs center-mass, inhale, exhale, steady. Even through a scope at almost two hundred yards, Arwen looks different, older, harder than she did just a few months earlier.

"Easy," says Charlie, who has a sixth sense for the mood of his oldest friend.

The collection of Indigenous warriors—Sioux, Apache, Cheyenne, Hopi, and Comanche, a force that might have altered the landscape of the American West if they had banded together centuries earlier—sits bareback astride horses along the crest of the dunes. Feathers affixed to spears, tomahawks, rifles, and braids fly horizontal in the wind.

Stone and Deuce stop twenty-five yards from the Sisterhood. Stone motions Mother toward them, and she strides to within a few feet, five Sisters at her side.

"Hey, baby girl," Deuce says to Arwen, around whose shoulder Mother, casually, menacingly, has draped an arm.

"*Hola*, Abuelo," Arwen says with a smile. "Missed you."

"Cut the crap," Mother hisses. "We're here to make a deal. Red for the whale."

"Understood," says Stone. "And accepted."

"Well?" Mother says.

Stone looks down, contemplative—classic Stone sandbagging—and kicks at the sand.

A spray of mist in the ocean comes first, an eruption of white foam forty feet high, then the leviathan. 52 Blue propels her four hundred thousand pounds out of the Gulf of Mexico with a single elegant whip of her tail. The largest mammal to live on planet earth levitates her full one-hundred-foot body above the water. She twists in midair, impossibly acrobatic, flashing her white belly, a single fin, and what can only be a smile, the smile of a mother seeing her newborn for the first time. And 52 Blue's heart, the entirety of her four-hundred-pound heart, belongs to one human and one human only, Arwen Laws, the redheaded thirteen-year-old girl on the beach with the razor-sharp blade of an Uncle Henry Hawkbill hard against her throat.

Mother smiles and squeezes Arwen's puerile left breast with her free hand. But the blade of the knife in her other hand doesn't move.

"First the whale," Mother whispers in Arwen's ear. "Then you."

Mother's trusted acolytes form a phalanx around their figurehead. In one voice, as the whale drops back into the water, they raise the battle cry of the Sisterhood, a shrill, bone-chilling ululation like the howl of something from Hell.

This is the moment of truth, that split second when a matador stands on his toes, sword poised over the shoulder of a defeated bull, and the crowd is as silent as a drifting feather. The moment of truth before the blade pierces the soft spot between the bull's powerful shoulder blades, down into his heart, and man and bull for a violent, beautiful moment become one.

A dot of red light appears on Mother's chest, and the crack of a gunshot pierces the silence. An acolyte dives in front of the Sisterhood leader just in time to stop the 170-grain round, which rips a dime-shaped hole in her lower back and blasts a puddle of viscera out of her abdomen like a nest of serpents. The phalanx of warriors tightens around Mother, and she draws the knife across Arwen's throat with enough pressure to draw a thin line of blood, but not enough to kill. Mother knows that the shooter will never risk the life of Arwen Laws.

"*Allahu Akbar,*" *God is great,* shouts Charlie Christmas. "One hundred and seventy yards. Not bad, Ranger."

"For shit," Ademar replies and chambers another round into her Henry lever-action .30-30. "Now what?"

A battle cry pierces the silence. A cloud of sand and dust rises in the distance, and out of it emerges a single rider, bareback astride a horse with red handprints on its flanks.

"White Cloud," Ademar whispers.

All stop. All hold their breath and turn to look at White Cloud. The old man seems transformed into the warrior of his youth, war paint on his face and body, feathered, beaded lance in one hand and reins in the other. The horse rises on its back legs and paws the air with its hooves. White Cloud lets out the ancient battle cry of the Sioux, leans low over the horse's neck, and charges.

All hell doesn't break loose. For a few seconds, Stone imagines a frieze, a moment of immortality painted on the side of an ancient urn: a lone warrior, one with his horse, lance in one hand and reins in the other, charging into impossible odds at a woman holding a knife on the neck of a child. But White Eagle has been carrying a secret that evens those odds. He knows Mother, knows the rapacious Sisterhood leader as Feather from the time he delivered her decades ago at Pine Ridge.

Everyone turns to look at White Eagle, except for one of the Sisters, who steps over the corpse of her compatriot and lunges at Deuce with a knife. The point of the blade digs deep into his chest, but not to the hilt. Star, who followed White Eagle into battle when he heard Arwen, covers the last ten feet to the Sister in one leap and grabs her wrist before the knife pierces Deuce's heart. In one graceful motion, no more than a second, Stone bends forward, pulls the commando knife from the holster around his ankle, and passes it across the Sister's jugular. Ademar fires four shots in rapid succession, and the remaining four warriors around Mother fall to the ground.

Mother, knife at Arwen's throat, stands alone as White Eagle reins his horse to a standstill in front of her.

"Feather," he says. "Stop! Stop this madness."

The split in Mother's veneer of invulnerability that first surfaced in front of the Sisters when Arwen defied their leader in the bull ring spreads across her face like a mudcrack on the high desert. Her acolytes sense it and shift uncomfortably, sending side-eye glances toward each other. Mother stammers at the imposing figure of the Lakota Sioux shaman towering above her on his stallion, a dark silhouette in the morning sun.

Mother is momentarily speechless, the radicalized zeitgeist of the powerful Sisterhood figurehead visibly seeping into the sand. "Wambleeska? White . . . White Eagle?" She straightens up, squares her shoulders in an attempt to regain the commanding footing so quickly yanked from underneath her at the sight of White Eagle. "I am Mother. Yes, yes, I am Mother." Nobody, least of all the Sisters behind her, are buying it.

"No!" White Eagle shouts, brandishing his spear in a wide arc over his head, his voice carrying over Mother to the befuddled Sisterhood warriors gathered behind their leader. "You are Feather, daughter of the Lakota Sioux nation, mother of Little Feather. I know! They should all know. I brought you into this world, Feather. I delivered your child, Little Feather. I healed you after the rape. But know this as clear as the sun behind me, I will snatch that precious life if you don't stop!"

An angel rests on one of Mother's shoulders, whispering *Feather*, and a devil on the other, screeching *Mother*. Her face contorts; her head jerks from side to side as if an electric shock is coursing through her body. Evil, tangible evil, wrestling for dominance with whatever good is left in her. A living, breathing manifestation of Gustave Doré's eighteenth-century masterpiece depicting Jacob struggling with an angel on the edge of a cliff.

Mother lowers the knife, eases her grip on Arwen.

Stone holds out his hand. "Come to me, baby girl."

Star, ears back and hackles up, crouches on her haunches, coiled to leap.

"Kill them," the devil hisses. "Remember the rape. The whale, everything, is within your reach."

"Save them," the angel replies. "Remember Little Feather. Free Arwen."

The angel seems to prevail. Mother drops the knife and releases Arwen.

Stone holds out his hand again. "Come to me, baby girl." And she does.

But evil never rests. The devil in Mother's imagination shouts, "Pocahontas!" All the memories—all the indignity, all the inequity, the rape, the death of Little Feather—pulse into her. Mother, the sociopathic tyrant, takes hold like a blue norther blowing across the Llano Estacado.

Mother jerks upright, a diabolical jack-in-the-box, whips the Glock from her belt, spins toward White Eagle, and fires. The Lakota warrior hurls his spear at the exact same moment. Time slows down. The entire universe, the Terra-Algorithm, the collective unconscious, pause to watch. This is the moment of truth. Humankind hangs in the balance. The bullet and the spear pass by each other, and both find their marks. Mother falls backward to the sand, spear tip through her heart. White Eagle, red streaks running from the hole in his chest, arches his back to sit upright on the horse. He looks to the horizon and sees a white buffalo, tilts his head upward to the sky, holds both arms out, and slumps forward, dead.

The battlefield yields to silence, to the wind and the rising tide drawing Mother's lifeless body into the ocean's embrace. But the fingers don't lift from triggers; the fists don't loosen around spears; and the steely resolve for battle, for victory or death, remains. The stillness is broken by the metallic click of

Sisters chambering bullets and a single warrior on the dunes shouting the ancient Sioux call to battle.

Ademar stands and fires a single shot into the air, and they all look to her. "Wait," she yells and points to a mass of people half a mile up the beach, running and closing fast.

Charlie shakes his head. "Mawiya, the Raramuri."

But it's not just him and his two dozen companions—enough, when combined with Ademar's forces, to prevail over the Sisterhood. Annie, who the Sisters know as Hecate, runs out front with Mawiya, matching him stride for stride. Everyone holds their fire, and their horses. The Raramuri come to a stop between the opposing sides, all of whom are now close enough to end the battle in hand-to-hand combat.

Annie steps forward. "Betty, our Sister Succubus, is dead," she says. "Hecate too."

"The fuck?" one Sister shouts. "That's you."

"Was me," Annie says. "*Was*. Betty talked about forgiveness, and she died defending us, from you. Forgiven. Hecate drowned, and Mawiya resurrected me, Annie. What were you before? What are you now? Mother is dead. Abandon the dark night of your souls."

"Join us," says Ademar, standing next to Annie. "The Free People of West Texas. The Indigenous Tribes. The Raramuri."

One of the Sisters lowers her weapon, then another and another, an act of submission to a new leader. Mother's second-in-command lays her weapon in the sand, walks to Ademar, and drops to one knee. "We surrender," she says, head bowed.

Ademar cups the Sister's chin in her hand and tilts it up firmly. "We don't take the knee," she says.

Ademar goes to Deuce, a mortal wound in his chest, barely alive. "Don't talk," she says. "Cap, what do you think?"

Stone is no doctor, but he's field-dressed his share of chest wounds. "I've seen worse," Stone says. "Thanks to the dog, I think Deuce makes it. Few more inches, different story."

"I was thinking about the last time at the stock tank. Rancho Seco," says Deuce, squeezing out a smile at Ademar.

"Rascal," Ademar says. "My old rascal."

"Where's Arwen?"

"Safe," says Ademar. "Where?"

The line of Sisters parts so Arwen can pass. Stone's knife in one hand, she walks into the ocean. The final act. What may be the last remaining blue whale on earth—the physical manifestation of the great journeys they have all made, the embodiment of the hopes they all have—floats half-submerged several hundred yards off the coast. The whale swims in as close as she can without beaching herself, and Arwen walks as far as she can on the sandy shelf. No stranger thing in their lives, touching what has only been a dream, a supernatural connection neither entirely understood but that neither could resist.

All eyes on the beach lock on the two figures in the ocean: the blue whale and the teenage girl from West Texas. They are not anticipating the fulfillment of a monomaniacal vision, but the end of a journey, littered with bodies, that could be the New Beginning for humankind. The girl and the whale touch, fin to hand, and the circle is complete.

Arwen climbs on the fin, scrambling over the whale's back to the lump and the scar behind her dorsal fin where Hannah Spencer embedded the hard drives. "This is gonna hurt, girl," Arwen whispers. 52 Blue seems to understand, stretches sideways so the skin is tight, easy to cut, and doesn't flinch when the blade reopens the old wound. "Easy," says Arwen, reaching up to her elbows into the wound and extracting a watertight plastic case the size of an airline carry-on. She stitches up the old wound as best she can with netting she found on the beach and cut into long strands. "It'll have to do, girl," Arwen says to the whale, who slaps the water and starts to sing. Arwen interprets the sudden sounds from 52

Blue, the favorite tune she's been clicking and humming for years, as agreement.

As soon as she slips off the whale's back and hops onto the sand bar, Arwen hears another sound, which at first she mistakes for 52 Blue's song. But it's not one whale; it's two in a divine undersea call and response. 52 Blue seems to smile at Arwen as she swims toward the other whale, a blue whale, the mate she's sought for decades. Another lost end connected; another circular journey in the universe complete.

52 Blue disappears underwater. From the beach, all they see is a thin young girl, a woman now, up to her waist on a sand bar in the Gulf of Mexico. During another time, before the Fall, she might have been bobbing on a raft with a dog paddling by her side. But there would not have been the two enormous whales breaching the surface in unison, belly to belly, fully out of the water and turning in midair, locking eyes first with Arwen, then with Ademar and those onshore. A wave washes over Arwen when the two whales crash to the surface, and they are gone.

CHAPTER 25

AFTER THE FALL

It has been decided. There will be no opening of the plastic case with the Toshiba hard drives until they reach Rancho Seco. For all the blood and treasure lost in the quest for the modern Holy Grail, not a single one of them really knows what to do with it. The digital infrastructure to reboot humanity is no longer a mouse click away, and Anonymous, which turned it all off in the first place, doesn't have the assets for the task, even if they are inclined to do so. In Mother's mind, having them and using them was the ultimate power. In Ademar's mind, preventing the hard drives from falling into the wrong hands, not using them, is the true power.

"Defense wins championships," says Stone, as most of the group—Free People, Sisters, Raramuri, Indigenous—survivors of what will be known to future generations as the Battle of Matagorda, makes their way on horseback to West Texas.

"He's right," says Deuce, nursing his chest wound supine in the back of a wagon pulled by a couple of mules. "And dammit, watch the bumps!"

"Possession is nine-tenths of the law," says Ademar, reins in hand, steering the buckboard with Deuce in back. "Don't need to decide anything until we see what's there."

It's a long ride from the balmy coast to the arid high desert of West Texas, seven hundred miles, but neither hard nor as dangerous now that the war is over. Weapons remain in their sheaths, and, increasingly as the miles pass, the former combatants break their cliquish formations to mingle and to share thoughts of the small things on the road. Very late in the season for bluebonnets, but heavy rains in the heart of the Hill Country just south of New Braunfels has the hills alive with the lavender blooms, the state flower of Texas. German immigrants settled in the Hill Country during the 1840s and brought with them their considerable skills brewing stout beer and smoking meats. The entourage weaves through the wreckage of small villages, microbreweries, and smokehouses left in the wake of the Fall, pulling up short a few hundred yards from a compound surrounded by a high stockade fence with guard towers in each corner. Smoke rises from a chimney in the middle, and music, polka music, drifts across the hills.

"Fucking kidding me?" T3 says.

"Sunday," says Deuce, rising on one elbow in the back of the wagon. "Germans."

"Lederhosen, cold beer, smoked sausage," says Stone.

"Don't count on it," says Ademar. "Stone, Charlie, Annie, let's check it out."

"I'm coming," says Arwen, not asking permission. "And Star."

"Good idea," says Deuce. "Nobody's gonna feel threatened by baby girl."

"If they only knew," Arwen says. "And, Abuelo, please stop calling me that."

"The rest of you hang back," says Ademar. "Way back, but not so far they can't see you."

Arwen cuts a small branch from a bigtooth maple and ties a piece of white cloth to one end, and the five of them, six counting Star, approach the stockade on horseback at a walk.

The music stops as a guard sounds an alarm from one of the towers. The riders hear the click of ammunition belts going into machine guns and stop. Before anyone can say anything, Arwen advances a few steps ahead of the others and waves the white flag.

"*Guten tag*," she says. "We're the Free People of West Texas. We come in peace."

"Where'd you learn that?" asks Stone.

"Jesus, Cap, everyone knows it," Arwen says.

"Must have been absent that day at Hebrew school," says Stone.

"What do you want?" says a man in the guard tower. "And who are those Indians behind you?"

"Nothing," says Arwen. "And those are our friends."

"Unless you can spare a little lunch," says Stone.

"Okay," the guard says, and the reinforced wooden gate opens. "Stay put. Nothing cute."

A small group walks out of the compound with a wooden table and a few benches, sets them down just outside the gate, and motions for them to join. The guards on the wall stay, and so do the gunners. Although they've been Americans and Texans for two hundred years, they are wearing traditional Bavarian outfits: lederhosen for the men and dirndls for the women. It's a Sunday, and traditions, especially after Armageddon when there's little else to hold on to, die hard. A surreal, almost comical scene in the midst of an apocalypse, but they all roll with it, and nobody would have been surprised if the Von Trapp family suddenly skipped out and burst into "The Sound of Music." Two rather large women with arms like prizefighters appear, three icy steins of beer in each fist, then two more with platters of sausage piled a foot high. The entire Free People entourage gathers around the table along with the Germans, and after several rounds of cold beer, sausage, sauerkraut, and pumpernickel slathered with spicy mustard, an old man playing the classic polka song "Schatzie" on an accordion strolls out of the compound.

A young man, about seventeen, approaches Arwen, who, after a beer, is feeling lighthearted and slightly lightheaded. "Dance?"

And they dance, first Arwen and the handsome young man, then all of them, prancing knees high, arms locked as if this were Oktoberfest in Munich and the world had not gone to shit. Arwen has never really danced, certainly not a polka, and for a few hours, a few precious hours, the trauma of the past few months seems like a distant memory. She is no longer a survivor, rather a teenage girl with a little beer buzz dancing joyfully alongside a handsome suitor. But the moment is short lived, and the party winds down with the setting sun.

"Thank you," says Ademar as they prepare to ride out. "Please visit us in Dell City."

"*Danke sehr*," Arwen says to the young man. "I'm Arwen. What's your name?"

"Heinrich. Call me Henry," he answers.

"Hope to see you again," she says.

"Me too," he says and kisses her on the cheek.

"All right then," Stone says. "Let's hit it."

The pentimento of that day seeps through the canvas of the long ride, reminding them of how it could be in the years ahead, that there might be a better future for modern civilization after the Fall. But there is no future without the past. Ademar and Deuce recall the darkness of their trip to Austin, the crucifixions and the carrion birds ripping at human flesh, as they ride past the twenty-one plaques commemorating the Uvalde mass shooting in 2022. Arwen wasn't even born when Salvador Ramos, a radicalized eighteen-year-old with two AR-15 assault rifles he bought a few weeks earlier, massacred nineteen kids and two teachers at Robb Elementary School. Outrage at the carnage of another mass murder in America, at the images of tiny, innocent children ripped beyond recognition by high-intensity bullets as they whimpered under desks, faded quickly in the news cycle and sagged under lobbying by the NRA and Trump sycophants on Capitol Hill who argued that more guns, not less, were the answer. But one woman, who was one of those kids in 2022, remembered that day every day since then. For that woman, who looked eighty but was barely forty, the Fall began the day she rubbed a classmate's blood on her body and played dead to avoid the madness of Ramos and the military-grade weapons he carried because it was his constitutional right. Ademar notices the woman's delicate fingers pulling weeds and placing flowers at the base of the twenty-one plaques, one for each innocent slaughtered that day, as they ride past.

"Remember?" Ademar says.

"Not for a long time," Deuce says.

"The beginning of the end," the woman, the survivor, says.

"Do you need anything?" Ademar asks her.

"No," she answers.

"Food, water, medicine?"

"I need an answer," she responds.

"There is no why," Stone answers. "Not for any of it."

"But there is hope," Arwen says. "Join us."

"Then who would tend this garden?" she replies. "I stay with my friends."

Forgotten is the afternoon with the Germans, the feeling of hope ahead for the world, as the Free People caravan winds its way the next week out of the Hill Country and into West Texas. The methodical click of horseshoes on the dry bed of the Pecos River echoes off the walls of the Seminole Canyon as they approach an immense cave shelter, known before the Fall as the Fate Bell, the size of an amphitheater with ancient murals painted on the towering, arched limestone walls. More than four thousand years before the Portuguese explorer Gaspar Castaño de Sosa discovered the Seminole Canyon pictographs, ancestral Puebloans made their home near the confluence of the Pecos and Rio Grande Rivers. With ample water, game, edible vegetation, and shelter, the canyon was an ideal spot for these Indigenous people, which included the predecessors of the Hopi, Pueblo, and Raramuri. By some estimates as old as ten thousand years, the pictographs may be the oldest known art of humankind, none more illustrative of ancient life and spirituality than the White Shaman mural. With its outstretched arms, the White Shaman, white because of the color of the limestone on which it's painted, is clearly a deity standing between what appears to be the foundation of their lives: land, agriculture, procreation, wildlife, and some form of tools or weapons. The Beginning. A perfect rendering of the interconnectivity of the universe, the Terra-Algorithm, Carl Jung's collective unconscious.

"If there is holy," Red Thunder, White Eagle's wife, says around the fire that night as she places a simple clay urn with his ashes at the base of the mural, "this is it."

"This is where we began," says Mawiya, taking a swig from a jug of *tesgüino*, the trademark corn beer of the Raramuri, and passing it around.

"As old as Moses," says Stone, pulling out the Cuban cigar White Eagle saved on the night before the Battle of Matagorda. "I wish he was here."

"He is," says Red Thunder, pointing the lit cigar Stone gives her at the White Shaman.

The journey is over. The story is told. All that's left, as they gather around the maze at Rancho Seco, is the opening of the box with the Toshiba hard drives. Ademar stands in the middle, surrounded by free people—West Texans, Raramuri, Indigenous Tribes, Sisters—those who chose to inherit the earth, not the wind. She pries open the hard case. It's empty, except for one piece of paper with a poem.

"Wild Geese"

You do not have to be good.
You do not have to walk on your knees
for a hundred miles through the desert repenting.
You only have to let the soft animal of your body
love what it loves.
Tell me about despair, yours, and I will tell you mine.
Meanwhile the world goes on.
Meanwhile the sun and the clear pebbles of the rain
Are moving across the landscapes,
over the prairies and the deep trees,
the mountains and the rivers.
Meanwhile the wild geese, high in the clean blue air,
are heading home again.
Whoever you are, no matter how lonely,
the world offers itself to your imagination,
calls to you like the wild geese, harsh and exciting—
over and over announcing your place
in the family of things.

—MARY OLIVER

EPILOGUE

2044: AFTER THE FALL

A rusting, barnacle-encrusted pile of oblong metal objects, bound with heavy metal chains around an enormous boulder, rests deep in an undersea cave off the Norwegian coast. A partial clue, the letter *T,* is still visible under the rust on one of them. A pod of dolphins, young and old, make this uncharted stretch of the Arctic Sea their home, along with three blue whales, one with a jagged scar behind her dorsal fin.

Only two humans have ever seen this cave: Hannah Spencer and her daughter, Azul. It is their secret. Hannah hid the objects there before the Fall, and what ensued as a result of her subterfuge was the greatest phony treasure hunt of all time.

During August, in the Land of the Midnight Sun, she and Azul visit the cave, swim with their undersea friends, and celebrate the survival of earth.

ACKNOWLEDGMENTS

And so it ends. The Lawses, the Zarkans, Stone, Charlie Christmas, and all the characters with whom I've lived every day the past four years hang up their spurs. The Seventh Flag trilogy is about journeys, of individuals, of a nation, and of a planet. Writing it was my journey. Those who accompanied me understand, and I am lucky they rode with me. Like the characters in the trilogy, my personal journey covered thousands of miles and ended in this magical slice of the world known as Far West Texas. The journeys of Ademar and her clan end now, but mine continues.

There are so many people to thank, starting with my personal cadre of readers, particularly Laura Payne, dean at Sul Ross State University, and Jonathan Wiedemann, Jack Price, and Bob Smith, lifelong friends. My thanks also to those—you know who you are—who have provided important guidance on the nuances of the story. Sending my thanks, but also my admiration, for the gifted Northern California artist Yvette Contois, who brought *Algorithms* and book two, *Murmuration*, to life with art for the cover that so perfectly captures the ethos of my novels.

There is, of course, a business side to all of this, and a bare-knuckle business it is. I could not have had a better guide for this journey than Brooke Warner, publisher at SparkPress and She Writes Press, the best indy around, and her team, particularly my personal project manager, Samantha Strom. No less important is the team that managed my publicity at Books Forward: President Marissa DeCuir and Lead Publicist Angelle Barbazon. It goes without saying that the independent bookstores, far too many to mention here, have played a significant role in the success of my novels. But special thanks to my friends Nancy Perot at Interabang Books in Dallas and Anne Calaway, Julie Green, and Rani Birchfield at Front Street Books in Alpine.

None of this would have happened without the support and friendship of the Schwartz and Smith families, icons of West Texas and guardians of the maze at the mythical Rancho Seco. The love of my children, Sidney and Mia, infuses my life and every word I write.

Finally, to my muse, Kleo Gabrielle Belay, alchemist of the Terra-Algorithm who conjured into the novel the pure magic of the natural world and its indigenous inhabitants, and helped guide the story down a true path.

And 52 Blue, a real whale, swimming free in the universe.

ABOUT THE AUTHOR

A Pulitzer-nominated national security correspondent and Writer in Residence at Sul Ross State University, Sid Balman Jr. has covered wars in the Persian Gulf, Somalia, Bosnia-Herzegovina, and Kosovo, and has traveled extensively with two American presidents and four secretaries of state on overseas diplomatic missions. After leaving daily journalism, he helped found a news syndicate focused on the interests of women and girls, served as the communications chief for the largest consortium of US international development organizations, led two progressive campaigning companies, and launched a new division at a large international development firm centered on violent radicalism and other security issues on behalf of governments. In addition to his current position as Writer In Residence at Sul Ross State University, Balman remains a working journalist and magazine contributor. A fourth-generation Texan, as well as a climber, surfer, paddler, and benefactor to Smith College, Balman lives in Alpine, TX, and has two children and a dog.

Author photo © Anneke D'Hollander, https://www.annekedhollander.be

SELECTED TITLES FROM SPARKPRESS

SparkPress is an independent boutique publisher delivering high-quality, entertaining, and engaging content that enhances readers' lives, with a special focus on female-driven work. www. gosparkpress.com

Murmuration: A Novel, Sid Balman Jr, $16.95, 978-1-68463-091-2. One of the first Muslim women to graduate from West Point, a Jewish US Army captain, and a Somali migrant nicknamed Charlie Christmas risk everything for a refugee boy on a three-decade odyssey that takes them from Africa and Europe to Texas and Minnesota—and redefines what it means to be American in the twenty-first century.

Seventh Flag: A Novel, Sid Balman, Jr. $16.95, 978-1-68463-014-1. A sweeping work of historical fiction, *Seventh Flag* is a Micheneresque parable that traces the arc of radicalization in modern Western Civilization—reaffirming what it means to be an American in a dangerously divided nation.

Hindsight: A Novel, Mindy Tarquini. $16.95, 978-1-943006-01-4. A 33-year-old Chaucer professor who remembers all her past lives is desperate to change her future—because if she doesn't, she will never live the life of her dreams.

Resistant: A Novel, Rachael Sparks. $16.95, 978-1-943006-73-1. Bacteria won the war against our medicines. She might be evolution's answer. But can she survive long enough to find out?

A Place Called Zamora: Book One, L B Gschwandter, $16.95, 978-1-68463-051-6. If an eighteen-year-old boy must risk his life in a motorcycle race to the very edge of a forty-story rooftop, his bike better be the one with brakes. That's what Niko faces in this dystopian story of love and survival: a race to the death that, if he survives it, will get him the girl of his choice and a kingdom of wealth laid out for him in an endless buffet. Except prizes like these come with strings in a city where corruption permeates everything, and there is no escape. Or is there?

Deepest Blue: A Novel, Mindy Tarquini. $16.95, 978-1-943006-69-4. In Panduri, everyone's path is mapped, everyone's destiny determined, their lives charted at birth and steered by an unwavering star. Everything there has its place—until Matteo's older brother, Panduri's Heir, crosses out of their world without explanation, leaving Panduri's orbit in a spiral and Matteo's course on a skid. Forced to follow an unexpected path, Matteo is determined to rise, and he pursues the one future Panduri's star can never chart: a life of his own.